SNAPS KE———————————————ERS

Snaps Kelly _____ r
in an equally _____
ordinary boy _____
cereals. But w_____ ...g stranger
than usual an__ _____ ...e turns dark blue with
silver stars all ov___, ne knows there must be an adventure
in store.

Then all the paper in London starts disintegrating, the
printers go out of business, there are no underground
tickets and daily life is changed dramatically. The evil
Dr Gripp is plotting to rid the world of paper but Snaps
and his friend Julie, with the help of Grandpa (which
isn't saying much), are hot on his trail. It looks as though
life in the civilized world could be destroyed for ever by
the Paper-Monsters . . .

Dr Joseph Ducke is a teacher in County Westmeath,
Ireland. He has written some school workbooks, but this
is his first novel. He is married with three children.

SNAPS KELLY
and the
Paper-Monsters

JOSEPH DUCKE

Illustrated by Terry McKenna

Puffin Books

For Aoife

PUFFIN BOOKS

Published by the Penguin Group
Penguin Books Ltd, 27 Wrights Lane, London W8 5TZ, England
Viking Penguin, a division of Penguin Books USA Inc.
375 Hudson Street, New York, New York 10014, USA
Penguin Books Australia Ltd, Ringwood, Victoria, Australia
Penguin Books Canada Ltd, 2801 John Street, Markham, Ontario, Canada L3R 1B4
Penguin Books (NZ) Ltd, 182–190 Wairau Road, Auckland 10, New Zealand

Penguin Books Ltd, Registered Offices: Harmondsworth, Middlesex, England

First published 1990
10 9 8 7 6 5 4 3 2 1

The moral right of the author has been asserted

Printed in England by Clays Ltd, St Ives plc
Filmset in Baskerville

Contents

— I —

Meet the Family

There were only two things in life that Snaps Kelly cared about. One was his grandfather, and the other was breakfast cereal. Snaps didn't just like breakfast cereal: he absolutely loved and adored it. And he didn't just love and adore one kind – he just loved them all. His only problem was that there were so many gorgeous tastes to be discovered and explored. Just when he thought he had come to the end of the lot, low and behold some new cereal would be launched which Snaps would add to his long list of others. While other kids went to record shops or toy shops or the museum in their spare time, Snaps liked to do nothing better than explore all the supermarkets in search of new cereal adventures. He would take a notebook along with him and add each new name to the list. At present he had one hundred and fifty names of different breakfast cereals. He would only have had one hundred and twelve were it not for the fact that he had recently started to explore the Indian and Greek and Pakistani self-service shops that cluttered the little side streets around Fitzroy Square in London where Snaps and his grandfather lived. Those ethnic shops were absolutely great. Each day it seemed that some new cereal was added to the long list of colourful boxes already lining the shelves. And what fantastic names they had: *Golden Coorg Flakes*, *Eastern Delight*, *Afghanabix*, *Persian Pops*. Snaps would saunter into each shop, stare up at the boxes, and take careful note.

His favourite shop was a small place off Goodge Street. It was called *The Cereal Store*, and was next door to a pork-shop called *Piggly-Wiggly*.

'Anything new for me today?' Snaps would say to old Mr Seymour who owned the store.

''Fraid so,' Mr Seymour would answer. 'This lot here arrived just this week.' And he would point to a new shelf-ful of multi-coloured boxes, all of which contained new delicious, scrumptious, delictacious breakfast cereals waiting to be gobbled.

'Oh no,' Snaps would say, as his eyes inspected the boxes. 'Where do all those breakfast cereals *come* from?'

'From *everywhere*,' Mr Seymour chuckled. 'Don't forget that this store sells every breakfast cereal in the *world*.'

Snaps sighed. His feelings were a mixture of delight and depression: delight when he considered all the glorious discoveries that still waited for him; depression when he thought of how long it would take him to get to the end of his ever-increasing list. The real problem was that he never seemed to make any real progress, for as soon as he discovered a new cereal, it became his favourite for a great length of time. At present he was

8

on his current favourite, a cereal called *Sugar Snaps*. In fact, he was a long time on *Sugar Snaps*, and this was only number thirteen on his list. But when he liked something, then he *really* liked it. He had eaten and enjoyed a dozen other cereals but had gradually got tired of them all. Then he discovered *Sugar Snaps*. They were great round rings in the shape of cartwheels and when you poured milk on them they really exploded. Yes, exploded! I don't mean the little timid noise that some cereals make, and that you have to turn your head sideways to hear. *Sugar Snaps* were a shattering experience, a mind-blowing, window-rattling, scintillating treat. The first time Snaps had *Sugar Snaps*, he just couldn't believe his ears. After pouring out the milk, he dived under the table until the worst of the noise was over, and his poor grandfather went running down the street to take refuge in the nearest tube-station.

'Look out!' Grandpa shouted to the confused commuters. 'There's an untamed breakfast cereal exploding in my kitchen.'

'Excuse me, sir,' said a traveller. 'Why are you wearing that World War II helmet? The war's over, you know.'

'Oh no it isn't,' snapped Grandpa. 'At this very moment the Dogs of War are destroying my kitchen.'

'Dogs?' said the ticket collector. 'Did you say dogs? I'm afraid we don't allow dogs on the trains, sir, unless they're accompanied by both parents. Too many dog fights lately . . .'

'Dog fights?' snapped Grandpa. 'Did you say *dog fights*?' He tipped his helmet sideways and listened for the *scheeeeaaaww* of fighting planes. But the only sound was of a train rumbling through the tunnel, like a submarine on wheels.

The train stopped, and Grandpa watched the people scramble aboard.

'Steady on,' he shouted. 'Women 'n' chislers first. You'll all be saved. You have *my* personal guarantee. We shall fight on the seas and on the oceans, we shall fight on the beaches, we shall fight in the fields and in the streets. We shall wring the neck of every chicken. We shall *never* surrender.'

Grandpa stopped. The train had gone. The underground station was silent. 'Sounds like the dog fight's over,' he said as he headed home to finish his breakfast, looking like an old soldier heading for Tipperary.

So, morning-time with Grandpa was an unpredictable adventure, especially when there were *Sugar Snaps* for breakfast.

Snaps and Grandpa soon got used to eating their *Sugar Snaps* while wearing goggles, helmets and flying gauntlets, all of which helped to cope with the exploding cartwheels, and with Grandpa's frantic antics.

Snaps had *Sugar Snaps* for breakfast, dinner and tea. And for supper as well. At school (whenever he went, that is) he had stopped taking a lunch, and would have a half-box of *Snaps* instead. This is why the other kids started calling him Snaps Kelly, and the name had quite easily stuck. Snaps didn't mind being called Snaps. In fact, he liked being called after his favourite breakfast cereal, and it was better than most names. He had got so used to his new name that when he was filling out the application form for his first job he had quite automatically put down Snaps Kelly instead of his real name. Even his grandfather, like everybody else, had taken to calling his grandson Snaps. Indeed, Snaps was sure that his grandfather no longer knew what his real name was!

Snaps loved his grandfather. He loved him the same as breakfast cereal and a little bit more than girls. But he liked girls as well. Grandpa Kelly had taken care of Snaps ever since his mother died. They lived on the top storey of a deserted building overlooking Fitzroy Square. They had lived there for years before anybody really knew about it. Then one day when the developers came to demolish the building, Grandpa Kelly openly announced his presence. Grandpa always seemed to be rushing into the street about something. On this occasion it was to claim his squatter's rights from the cranedriver who sat high up in the air dangling a huge iron ball over the scrawny old gentleman who had unexpectedly appeared beneath him.

'Hey,' Grandpa shouted. 'Take your ball and play somewhere else. This is a nice neighbourhood and we don't want you to break our windows.'

A crowd of polite Londoners gathered to applaud Grandpa's speech on human rights, civil rights and any other rights you care to mention, though nobody could really hear him because of the noise of the crane. In any case, demolition of the building was temporarily halted until a court decision was attained, and the big crane lumbered away again like a great sad dinosaur.

If Grandpa Kelly had one fault, it was that he could never really stay out of trouble. Nor could he find anything to interest him for very long. His interests and hobbies were constantly turning, twisting, and changing. Soon after he had saved the house from demolition, he had decided to do a survey on the cats in Fitzroy Square.

'It's a curious thing,' Grandpa said to Snaps one morning after breakfast. 'There are catalogues filled with facts about the catacombs; there are – I'm almost certain – boring books on catamarans and catapults; there are – no doubt – beastly books about cataracts, catarrh and other catastrophes. There have even been surveys of the hairy caterpillar. But there are no surveys of the cats in Fitzroy Square.'

'Oh?' said Snaps. 'So what do *you* hope to prove?'

'Prove?' said Grandpa. 'I hope to prove lots of things. There are lots of false notions about cats, you know. I hope to put the record straight. For example, what's the old saying about cats and curiosity?'

'Curiosity killed the cat,' Snaps said.

'Well, that saying is wrong,' said Grandpa. 'It's as wrong as spots on a zebra. It wasn't curiosity that killed the cat, it was *gravity*.'

'And that's what you hope to prove?'

'Among other things, yes.'

'Not much, is it?' said Snaps.

'But that's just the beginning,' said Grandpa, grinning like the cat that swallowed the canary.

After collecting all the necessary equipment (nets, whips, a camouflage suit and some fake mice), Grandpa set about surveying the Fitzroy cats who, it soon became obvious, did not wish to be surveyed at all. At all hours of the day and night, he could be seen chasing after elusive felines, or standing still in his cat-suit, mice and net at the ready waiting for a casual cat to appear. His energy was mostly directed towards a huge tom-cat whom he called Fitzroy. Snaps wasn't quite sure what Grandpa intended to do with Fitzroy if ever he caught him. Perhaps he intended to mount his head over the fireplace. Still, Snaps was sure of one thing: there was no danger of Grandpa ever capturing Fitzroy even if he tried for the rest of his life. In any case, his cat period came to a sudden and unexpected end. One evening in pursuit of Fitzroy, Grandpa climbed a tree, one of those big ones at the edge of the Square. Unfortunately, this tree also happened to be outside the bathroom of Ms Whetstone, who was sitting in her bath just as Grandpa's bony head appeared above the window-sill.

'*Aaaaaaggghhhhhh*,' she screamed.

Fitzroy jumped, and Grandpa tumbled to the ground. Whatever about gravity killing cats, it very nearly killed Grandpa that day.

In the court-case which followed, Ms Whetstone called Grandpa 'an old snooper'. He replied that he would prefer a nice pork chop from *Piggly-Wiggly*'s rather than a lump of wasted old mutton like her. The judge hammered his gavel.

'Order, order,' he shouted. 'That's no way to address a lady.'

'Sorry, yer 'onour,' said Grandpa, 'but I never take orders from judges unless they're sober.'

The judge's face went dark with rage.

'Are you suggesting that I'm *not* sober?'

'Well, now that you mention it,' said Grandpa, 'you *do* seem a little green about the gills. You *do* look weak and sickly. Let's just say that if you were a horse, you would probably have to be shot . . .'

'I didn't come here to be insulted!' said the judge.

'No?' said Grandpa. 'Where do you usually go?'

Needless to say, the judge fined Grandpa twenty pounds for that piece of cheek, and another twenty for insulting Ms Whetstone.

'I refuse to pay,' Grandpa said.

'OK then,' said the judge. 'Let's make it fifty.'

Grandpa was about to let fly another skit of words when Snaps kicked him under the table. Grandpa's mouth snapped shut like a book. He slumped down into his chair like an airborne paper kite that had suddenly run out of wind.

Grandpa was in a very sour mood after this defeat. As he and Snaps walked across the city he was muttering vexedly to himself. It was one of those gorgeous July evenings when the sky was a blaze of colour above the roof-tops. They had sat in Fitzroy Square until it was almost dark, watching the cats play in the late evening sunshine. But Grandpa took no interest in them. When he and Snaps finally went home, a big surprise awaited them. On the top of the stairs right in front of their door sat a big tom-cat, with a big grin across his face. It was Fitzroy. Grandpa took one look at him and said, 'A fine mess you got me into!' By the expression on his face Fitzroy seemed to answer: 'Serves you right!' Both of them agreed to call a truce. When Snaps and Grandpa opened the door, Fitzroy casually followed them inside as if he and Grandpa Kelly had never been enemies. From then on he became a house cat instead of a wild cat, and he cleaned up all the mice in the old shaky building. That was how Fitzroy became one of the family.

Grandpa's cat period was slightly less bothersome than his snooker period. It was the time of the snooker craze in Britain and Grandpa had decided that it was time he learned how to play. When Snaps came home from school one day he was amazed to find a huge snooker table sprawled across the living-room. There was just about enough room to walk around it. The room had been darkened and there in the twilight was Grandpa Kelly chalking a cue. He was dressed in a black waistcoat, an old-fashioned dickie-bow, but no shirt.

'How do I look?' Grandpa said as he snapped the sides of his dickie-bow. 'Pretty neat, eh?'

For the next few weeks he rarely left the snooker table, except at mealtimes or when he got too tired and had to get some rest. Yet even then, Snaps would often awake at night to hear the sound of snooker balls clipping each other and the delighted squeals of Grandpa Kelly from the other room.

'Playing snooker is like walking on your eyeballs,' Grandpa said to Snaps as he took careful aim. He had twisted his body into a giant question mark, and his chin was almost touching the table.

'Really?' said Snaps.

'Oh yes, really,' Grandpa continued. 'It has very little to do with arms and elbows. Though, of course, there *is* something else you need.'

'Oh? And what would that be?'

'A lot of neck,' Grandpa said.

One day when Snaps came home from school, Grandpa had moved the snooker table on to the second floor of the building where he had much more room to practise. A funny thing about Grandpa Kelly, he always seemed to get things done when Snaps was out. This was always a source of amazement to Snaps. He knew that Grandpa couldn't have moved the table himself, any more than he could have done any of the other weird things he got up to. Snaps had only to leave the house for a few short hours, and when he got back he would notice some great transformation in the arrangement of things. A new staircase would have been constructed leading nowhere in particular, a new window might be facing on to the street, or a large motorcycle might be parked casually beside the bed. Yet Grandpa would continue about his business as if nothing at all had happened. At first Snaps would always ask Grandpa where all this stuff came from.

'OK, Grandpa. How do you do it?'

'How do I do what?' Grandpa sounded as innocent as a child in a china-shop.

'You know what I mean,' Snaps said. 'Where does all this stuff *come* from?'

But extracting information from Grandpa was like pulling bent rusty nails from old timber.

He would only give his cute grin and say: 'Ask no questions, get told no lies!' And Fitzroy would grin up at Snaps as much as to say: 'Serves you right for asking!'

In order to build up his stamina for playing snooker, Grandpa had taken to jogging. He and Snaps would head off for Regent's Park at some unearthly hour, and Grandpa would run off into the distance, half-hidden in the mist of the early morning. He was a funny spectacle in his long shorts and skinny legs with their varicose veins standing out like the River Ganges. Snaps would sit on the seat near the west-side gate with the stop-watch ticking away. Sometimes Grandpa was a long time. All the other trim joggers with their colourful sweat-bands and sun-tanned legs would have finished for at least an hour before Grandpa finally appeared at the turn of the big hedge, panting, spluttering and groaning. 'How did I do?' he'd ask, as soon as he had got his breath back. 'Quite good,' Snaps would say, trying to be encouraging. 'But not good enough,' Grandpa would always answer. 'I'll be faster tomorrow.'

As soon as he was good enough, Grandpa entered all the small snooker competitions in the West End. And he did remarkably well. He didn't so much beat his opponents as kill them with boredom. Grandpa's tactic was always to slow the game down to a snail's pace. He would walk round the table a hundred times eyeing each of the balls with the expression of a hawk eyeing a mouse, and mumbling quietly to himself.

He also composed little lines of poetry so as to help his concentration:

'The white looks right, and the blue will do;
First the brown and then the green.
We all live in a yellow submarine . . .'

Then just as he was shaping up for a shot and everyone thought he had finally made a decision, he would suddenly stop, reconsider, and then set off on his rambles again. When his opponent eventually got a chance at the table, Grandpa would let out coughs, sneezes, or loud shouts of encouragement –

'Yipee! Go for it, m' lad. Don't be nervous, now. Don't mind all those people looking at you. And don't just tickle that white ball. Really *smack* it.

'Show no mercy,
Show your pace.
Knock that ball about the place!'

– with the result that his distracted opponent missed

the simplest of shots. Then it was Grandpa's turn once more, and the long walk round the table began all over again.

It was tactics such as these that won Grandpa a place in the Amateur West-End Snooker Final held every year in a large hotel in Russell Square. And what an affair that turned out to be. His opponent was a long gangly youth called Ted Clifford, who was a senior boy at Snaps's school. Snaps didn't care much for Ted Clifford. Grandpa liked him even less. The entire event was a fiasco right from the start. First, Grandpa insisted on taking Fitzroy into the hotel as a good-luck charm. He had dressed Fitzroy in a white collar and dickie-bow, and when the doorman of the hotel told Grandpa that they didn't allow 'vermin' inside, Grandpa kicked up an awful stink.

'Did you say "vermin"?' said Grandpa. There was a purposeful set to his jaw, and the light from his eyes was harsh and cold, like chips of broken glass. Snaps knew that a storm of rage was coming.

'I'll have you know that this cat is a distant relative of Dick What's-his-name's famous feline who went to London to see the Queen. This cat's great grandfather once worked for Harry Houdini. This cat has had more escapes than a monkey's uncle, and has gobbled more mice than you've had dinners. So step aside, like a good man.'

Eventually, the matter was settled and Fitzroy was allowed to stay, though Snaps had to keep him on a lead. The game started one hour late because Grandpa had mysteriously 'disappeared'. Actually he was hiding in one of the plush bathrooms, and this was a plan he often used to unsettle his opponent. As soon as the match began it was obvious that the refereeing was going to be strict. Each time he coughed, sneezed, shouted, or spilled his water he was severely cautioned by the referee. The chief umpire fined him ten points for obvious time-wasting, and when Grandpa called him 'an old grouch', the umpire fined him a further five. Half-way through the match, the game had to be halted to allow Ted Clifford to change his shirt after Grandpa 'accidentally' dropped three ice-cubes down the back of his neck. During the break which followed, Grandpa was caught moving the pink ball to a less easy position, and he was fined ten pounds for bringing the game into disrepute. When Grandpa's turn finally came, the umpire had to ask him on several occasions would he mind not leaving his cigar on the edge of the table because he was destroying the surface.

Then Grandpa noticed that the black ball had a little white window of reflected light. He bent down, examined it closely and said to the attendant:

'I don't like the way that black ball is grinning at me. Would you please wipe that grin off its face.'

The attendant wiped the black ball in his white gloves and replaced it carefully on to the table.

But in the end, Grandpa had to settle for the runner's-up trophy. Ted Clifford's victory might have been faster were it not for the fact that the black ball mysteriously disappeared. Soon it was discovered that Grandpa was hiding it in his pocket, and the match was awarded to Clifford. Just as Grandpa was about to accept his trophy, a steward pointed out that he had still not paid his entrance fee, and when Grandpa refused to do so, his trophy was withdrawn. He was also banned from the game of snooker for 'a period of forty years', but Grandpa said he didn't care because he had other plans for the next forty years anyway. When Snaps, Grandpa and Fitzroy left the hotel, they noticed that Ted Clifford's motorbike was parked outside. So they let the air out of the back tyre and continued happily on their way. That was the end of Grandpa Kelly's snooker period.

But it wasn't the end of his getting up to mischief. Grandpa Kelly had always reckoned he was an artistic person, and no sooner had his snooker period ended than his artistic period began. One morning he said to Snaps:

'The world is full of artists, dabblers and messers. The messers mess, and the dabblers merely dabble. But the artist is neither a dabbler nor a messer.'

With this famous announcement, Grandpa Kelly's artistic period began.

And this period was the most secretive of all. Even Snaps didn't discover what he was up to until it was almost too late. Every morning Grandpa Kelly would head off on the bus or the underground for the Tate or the National Portrait Gallery or some such place dressed in the smock and loose hat of a genuine artist. There he would survey the various paintings, deciding which were good and which were not.

'Hmmm. This one is not particularly good,' he would say to himself as he examined some well-known masterpiece.

Once he had decided that a painting was not particularly good, he immediately set about improving it. In the early hours just after opening time, when the steward had moved off to the other end of the room, Grandpa would sneak a little box of paints from under his smock. Then he would 'improve' some priceless painting by adding a moustache, a grin, a beauty spot or a set of spectacles. He was in the process of adding a bikini and sunglasses to Botticelli's naked Venus before he was eventually discovered. And then all hell broke loose. Sirens and alarms burst into a dismal chorus of noise, yet Grandpa continued painting as if nothing had happened.

'A true picture restored,' said Grandpa, as he stepped back to admire his masterpiece.

He had even changed the signature from Botticelli to Bottikelly (though some people thought later that *Dotty*kelly would have been even more appropriate).

He was immediately arrested by three hefty guards, while a fourth took hold of his skinny legs to try to stop him from kicking.

'Don't make such an exhibition of yourself,' one of the guards shouted as Grandpa struggled to get free.

'Why not?' answered Grandpa. 'I thought art galleries were meant for exhibitions.'

He was taken away to a back room where he was questioned by a collection of small baldy men with small tummies sticking out over their trousers. One of them kept saying 'Dear me! Dear me! This is terrible! This is absolutely terrible!'

'But no,' said Grandpa. 'It's quite a good job I've done, even if I do say so myself.'

'Do you have any statement to make?' asked the curator of the gallery, and his voice was as hard as old boots.

'A statement?' said Grandpa. 'Let me see . . . "The cat is on the mat". That's a statement isn't it? "Can I have a cup of tea with two sugars, and a slice of cherry-cake from the cafeteria, if there's any left?" That's another statement, isn't it? Or was that one a question? Oh yes, I think I see a question mark at the end . . .'

To make matters worse, Grandpa refused to tell which paintings he had tampered with, so an expert had to be flown in from America to examine every single painting in the gallery. The whole place was closed down for two months while the paintings were closely checked for signs of Grandpa Kelly's handiwork. In the court-case which followed (Grandpa was becoming quite a regular visitor to court rooms) Grandpa's lawyer told him to plead insanity, which wasn't very difficult for Grandpa, though he was slightly offended at the idea. In any case, he was fined £100 for acting in a criminal manner, and he was banned from the Tate for a period of fifty years. That was the end of Grandpa Kelly's artistic period.

As for Snaps, life with Grandpa was becoming a little bit too exciting for his liking. No sooner had they got over one mess than Grandpa would get involved in another. Snaps had never really left school. He just didn't seem to have any time to go. He spent most of his day supervising Grandpa's latest project, or going with him to court-cases, and things like that. Also, with all the fines Grandpa was accumulating in one way or another, Snaps felt that he himself should make some effort to pay some of the bills. So he got a job. It was with a small printing firm called Pilkington Publishers Ltd that was situated at the corner of Fleet Street. The firm also dealt in old and antiquarian books, and it delivered consignments of new books to bookshops and libraries. Snaps was employed as a delivery boy. The firm had, of course, a delivery van as well. But Snaps was used for short runs and for small deliveries. He had also to deliver parcels that were needed in a hurry, and his small moped could weave its way through the London traffic much faster than the company van. Though the job was for the summer period only, Snaps hoped that Mr Pilkington might see his way to make Snaps a permanent employee in the firm.

The business was expanding rapidly, and it was quite probable that extra employees would be needed fairly soon. Variety was the secret of Mr Pilkington's success, and nothing was too humble for him to print: football programmes, tourist brochures, catalogues, leaflets of all sorts, bingo cards, student magazines, raffle tickets, invitation cards, in fact just about everything. And when you added to these the steady trade in old and antiquarian books, well it looked like the future of Pilkington Ltd was very secure indeed. True, there had been a bad period after the war when it was hard to get spare parts for the old printing-presses. But that was a long, long time ago, and Pilkington's had been steadily growing since then. Mr Pilkington thought of the company as a kind of monument to his father's memory. He tried, as much as possible, to keep everything just as it had been in his father's time. He had even refused to change the old-fashioned hand-painted sign that hung above the door.

It was now early in June, that time of year that every young person loves. It was really perfect weather for riding round London on a moped. The sun, like a well-loved pop-star, continued to make personal appearances daily. The city was alive with smiling tourists, giggling boys and colourful girls.

Snaps set his alarm clock for seven-thirty, as he had to be at Mr Pilkington's shop before nine. He liked to arrive before everybody else, so that Mr Pilkington could see what a keen worker he was. Usually, however, Snaps had no need of the alarm clock to wake him up, for Grandpa was always up before him, rummaging, muttering, and making plenty of noise. On this particular morning, Snaps was disturbed by Grandpa's loud squeals that seemed to be coming from the roof. Snaps got up quickly and went out on to the flat roof on top of the building. Sure enough there was Grandpa jumping excitedly beside a large telescope that was pointed at the morning sky. One solitary star hung over London in a sky that was as charming as a multi-coloured parasol. But Grandpa wasn't looking at the star; he was looking in horror at something else. Snaps followed the direction of his gaze.

'I knew it!' Grandpa was shouting. 'I just knew this would happen! Just as soon as they got my back turned, they landed in that atrocious rocket!'

'But Grandpa, that's not a rocket,' Snaps said. 'That's the Post-Office Tower.'

Grandpa stopped jumping. His eyes narrowed into tiny slits as he thought for a moment about what Snaps had said.

'The what?' he asked in a hushed voice.

'The Post-Office Tower,' Snaps said again.

'And how long has that been there?'

'I don't know exactly,' Snaps answered, 'but a pretty long time, I suppose.' 'Then how come no one told *me*

24

about it? How come nobody ever tells me *anything* any more?' He was walking wildly round the telescope and was throwing his arms in the air.

'Oh, Grandpa,' Snaps said, 'maybe that's enough star-gazing for one day. Shouldn't you get some rest?' Grandpa said nothing; he just went back inside, muttering quietly to himself. Snaps followed him inside, and started preparing breakfast: two bowls of *Sugar Snaps*, some orange juice and a pot of tea. Grandpa was never very talkative in the morning, so they ate their breakfast without talking. When they had finished, Snaps quickly washed up, and taking some *Sugar Snaps* and a carton of milk with him for lunch, he headed off to work.

'See you later, Grandpa,' Snaps called out as he headed down the stairs.

'So long, son,' Grandpa answered, 'have a nice day at school.'

As he passed the snooker room, Snaps noticed that the snooker table was completely changed. It was no longer green, but had instead a dark blue surface with little silver stars. Instead of snooker balls, there were spheres of different colours and sizes, on which the names of different planets were marked in bright golden paint. Over the door the name *Snooker Room* was crossed out, and *Galaxy Room* was put in its place.

Snaps rushed back upstairs, taking two steps at a time. Grandpa was sitting looking out of the window with Fitzroy on his lap.

'How did the snooker room get changed so fast?' Snaps asked. But Grandpa just gave his cute grin and said: 'Ask no questions, get told no lies!' And even Fitzroy smiled like someone who knew all about it, but who wasn't prepared to tell. As Snaps headed off to work, he wished that life would get a little less exciting. All he wanted was a long peaceful summer, free from all disturbance. But little did he realize the adventure that lay in store for him . . .

— 2 —

Enter Doctor Samuel Gripp

Snaps loved London, but he loved it most early in the morning. He set off for Fleet Street on his moped with a warm breeze blowing his hair.

'I hope Grandpa will be OK,' he thought to himself. 'He's been acting rather stranger than usual lately.'

He crossed the big crossroads at Tottenham Court Road. This was one of his favourite streets, because it reminded him of his favourite football team. Mr Pilkington had told him always to take the shortest way to a place so as to save time, for time was very important to a businessman.

'The shortest distance between two points is a straight line,' Mr Pilkington said to Snaps one morning. 'But a short-cut is even shorter than that.'

Snaps now knew many short-cuts, because he had been working for Mr Pilkington for almost three weeks and had seen an awful lot of London in that time. He'd also learned a lot of short-cuts from Grandpa, ones that involved crashing through red lights or driving down one-way streets, so he didn't use these very often, only in emergencies.

Soon he arrived at Mr Pilkington's shop in Fleet Street, and as usual, he was first. He parked his moped and sat on the window-sill waiting for the others to arrive. Altogether, there were seven people working at Pilkington's. Firstly, there was Mr Pilkington himself who had been in the business for many years and who knew an awful lot about books and printing. Once, Mr Pilkington asked Snaps if he knew the difference between a good book and a bad newspaper; while Snaps was searching his brain for an answer, Mr Pilkington said:

'A bad newspaper separates the sense from the rubbish and then prints the rubbish. But a good book prints only the sense.'

Mr Pilkington liked to say clever things. 'But what about a bad book?' Snaps was wondering, but he didn't bother to ask. On his desk Mr Pilkington had a sign which said: *The Book Stops Here*. Snaps thought to himself: 'That must be that big book that Mr Pilkington is always writing in, and that Miss Creef is always losing.'

Miss Creef was Mr Pilkington's secretary. She was a real scatter-brain. Most days she arrived at work dressed like a bag of washing. She rarely wore shoes that matched, and she was never on time. Whenever Mr Pilkington asked her where she had been, she would answer with a sigh:

'I'm afraid Mildred was very troublesome this morning.' Or else she would say that she had performed a great act of charity by visiting a lonely friend. Mr Pilkington would just shake his head and mutter something to himself. One day he said to Snaps:

'That woman is so complicated she could make a straight line seem like a corkscrew.'

The office was kept tidy by a nice young lady called Agnes. She was always happy and cheerful, and Snaps liked her a lot. She also made the tea, and did most of the things that Miss Creef was supposed to do. Mr Henry, the chief printer, was rather a quiet man who kept mostly to himself. He drove a little Morris Minor car which he parked in Whitefriars Street, just round the corner from Pilkington's. Mr Henry had been a printer at Pilkington's for nearly forty years, and he once told Snaps that whenever he couldn't sleep at night, he counted letters instead of sheep. His favourite game was *Scrabble* and his favourite food was alphabet spaghetti which, he said, made him a very good speller, and it was very important for a printer to be a good speller. He also invented new words of his own, words like *dillgogreous*, which meant very gorgeous, and *gorgeocious*, which meant very gorgeous indeed. He had once said that Agnes was 'a gorgeocious person' but that Miss Creef wasn't 'very dillgogreous at all'. Printing was not just a *job* to Mr Henry: it was his pride and joy. He had always done his best for the company, right from those early days when he had arrived as an office-boy, and had first heard the strange clack of the Monotype machines. He loved the company, the clattering noise, the papery dust and the secret language of printers. And he loved the basic stuff of the trade: the clean-cut sheets of immaculate paper, and the dark, spidery, magical printers' ink.

'You know,' he said to Snaps one day during tea-break, 'I've been around the world in less than eighty days, and I still managed to meet everybody twice. I'm also the only person, living or dead, who knows an English word that rhymes with *orang-utan*.'

Whenever Mr Pilkington asked Mr Henry to do some overtime on Saturday, Mr Henry always refused.

'I will work any day except Saturday,' he'd say. 'After all, it's only fair. Even Friday got Saturday off, thanks to Robinson Crusoe.'

Mr Henry's assistant was a boy called Iain, who spent most of his time thinking about Agnes, or smoking cigarettes in the back store-room. Iain was tall and bushy-haired, with long narrow teeth. He had also the funniest laugh that Snaps had ever heard. It was a sort of long 'Haw-Haw-Haw' sound like a donkey makes. Iain's laugh made Snaps laugh more than Iain's silly jokes. During lunch-time, Iain often played *Scrabble* with Mr Henry, and they had constant arguments about some of Mr Henry's words:

'There is no such word as *codology*. Or *bulltripe* . . .'

'There is.'

'Isn't . . .'

Finally, there was Bill Heap, the van driver. He chewed gum constantly, and Iain was always trying to cadge some off him. Bill Heap would tell Iain to give up chewing-gum or his teeth would stop growing, but Iain would answer that they had grown quite enough already. Bill had not much interest in printing, publishing, or books. He would dump the loads of parcels into the back of the van as if they were bales of hay, and Mr Pilkington was always telling him to be careful because books were precious items. Bill always said that he

would be more careful in future, but when Mr Pilkington wasn't looking he'd continue loading the van in
the same rough way. Also, he was constantly forgetting
to get the dockets signed, and there were often rows in
the office over this.

It was a beautiful morning in June as Snaps sat on the
window waiting for the others to arrive. The buses had
started to roll, and crowds of busy people were heading
off to their different places of work. Suddenly, Snaps's
attention was attracted by a tall dark gentleman who
had just emerged from the underground tube-station
across the street. He was dressed in a beautiful white
suit, a white shirt, and dark-coloured tie. He was also
wearing very thick spectacles which didn't really suit
him. Snaps wondered what a person like that might
work at, but then he didn't seem to be in any sort of
hurry to get to work at all. With his watch-chain,
walking-stick and briefcase, he looked like a professor of
some sort, or one of those brainy-looking people that
Snaps had often seen hurrying into the British Museum.
But this man was in no hurry. He just sauntered down
the far side of the street as if he was out for a morning
stroll.

'Good morning, Snaps,' a voice said. It was Mr
Pilkington. 'I see you're early as usual.'

Snaps was quite pleased with this remark. 'Yes, sir,'
he answered cheerfully, 'I always like to be early.' Mr
Pilkington fumbled with the big bunch of keys. He
unlocked the security door, then the main door, and
they both went inside. Presently, the others arrived
(except for Miss Creef of course) and soon the place
was a buzzing hive of activity. The huge printing-

machine clicked and hummed in the background, while Agnes sorted out the bundles of parcels that had to be delivered that day. Bill Heap took the bigger bundles and threw them into the back of his van, while Snaps gathered up the smaller parcels, which he placed in the special carrier on the back of his bike. Snaps usually didn't leave until after the postman had come, just in case there were any special requests for deliveries. In the mean time, he did odd jobs around the store, tidying the reams of paper, sorting through the shelves of antiquarian books to check that they were all in order, running errands, or simply sweeping up.

'Hey, Snaps!' Mr Pilkington called, as Snaps was carrying a huge roll of paper out to Mr Henry. 'I want you to make a deposit at the bank. We have a lot of cash on hand and it just isn't safe to leave lots of money lying around.' Snaps went into the office and got his orders from Mr Pilkington. Usually it was Agnes who went to the bank, but she had extra work to do because Miss Creef still hadn't arrived.

As Snaps went down the street towards Lloyds, he noticed that the well-dressed gentleman he had seen earlier was leaving Mr Webster's shop. Mr Webster was a dealer in old and very rare postage stamps. Indeed, it was said that he had the oldest and best collection of stamps in Britain, older and better than the stamps in the British Museum. Before he continued down the street, the gentleman stopped for a moment and stared closely at the old battered stamp album that lay on display in Mr Webster's shop window. The sign said, *Priceless Stamps: The Oldest Collection in the World*. Then the gentleman walked off quickly, and disappeared among the crowd of hurrying people on the busy street.

When Snaps returned from the bank, there was great excitement outside Mr Pilkington's office. Mr Pilkington was holding up a very important-looking letter that the postman had just brought, and he was smiling from ear to ear. Agnes, Mr Henry and Bill Heap had all gathered round, and Iain had just come from the store-room, smelling of tobacco.

'Ah, Snaps,' said Mr Pilkington, 'you're just in time to hear the good news!' He cleared his throat with a short cough, and with one hand on his waistcoat, and the other holding the letter, he continued.

'I have here a letter from Her Majesty the Queen.' (There were sudden gasps and intakes of breath.) 'You know that each year Her Majesty invites all the old soldiers of World War II to a big tea-party in her garden. Well, this year she wants Pilkington Publishers Ltd to print the invitation cards.'

'Gee!' said Agnes.

'Oh boy!' said Mr Henry.

'Wow!' said Bill Heap.

'You're kidding!' said Iain.

'I bet my grandfather will be invited to that!' Snaps said proudly. 'He's an old soldier of the war. In fact, he's an old soldier of a lot of wars!'

'Well, make sure you tell him where the invitation cards came from,' said Mr Pilkington with a broad smile. 'Oh! I'm so happy to think that her Majesty should have chosen us! I'm so happy . . . I could . . . I could . . . *kiss someone!*'

Everyone took a step backwards.

'Try *me!*' a voice said from behind them. It was Miss Creef, arriving to work at last. She was dressed in a red velvet dress, a straw hat and a pair of Adidas runners.

Everyone suddenly scattered, not wanting to get involved in the big row that was sure to follow. But Mr Pilkington was in much too good a humour to be upset by Miss Creef arriving late yet another morning. He just rubbed his small moustache, and told everyone to get busy because there was a lot of work to be done. Then, taking a look at Miss Creef he shook his head and cast his eyes up to the ceiling before walking back into his office.

Snaps gleefully headed off on his rounds. It was a beautiful sunny morning and London was a dazzle of colour. His first stop was a library in St Pancras. He loved going there because his bike could pick up tremendous speed on the straight stretch along Euston Road. He zipped past the big building with the mirrors, past the train station and the fire brigade, and then down the long, wonderful, slope to St Pancras library. He hadn't many deliveries to make really, so there was no need to be in such a hurry. Still, he liked going fast just for the heck of it.

There was nobody at the library desk when Snaps went inside, so he rang the small bell that said 'Please Ring'. The library was deserted, except for one person whom Snaps couldn't see, and who was rummaging behind some far shelves. Presently, a bright young girl appeared from the back office. She was blonde, smiling and good-looking.

'Yes?' she said. 'Can I help you?'

Snaps's attention had wandered slightly at the sight of her.

'Can I help you?' she said again.

'A delivery from Pilkington Ltd,' Snaps blurted out

34

at last. He handed over the parcel of books. He could not take his eyes off her.

'Aren't you rather young to be a librarian?' he said.

'Aren't you rather cheeky to be a delivery boy!' she answered with that same gorgeous smile (Mr Henry would have said *dillgogreous*) and they both laughed. 'Actually, if you must know, I'm not a librarian. This is just a summer job, sort of work experience, you know.'

Snaps was leaning on the desk, gazing into her eyes. *Gorgeocious*, most definitely.

'Are you waiting for something in particular?' the bright young girl then asked. Snaps produced a docket from his pocket. 'I've got to have this signed,' he said.

'OK,' she answered cheerily, and went back into the office.

While he was waiting, Snaps twiddled with the jar of coloured pencils that was on the desk. Suddenly there was a loud thud of falling books from behind him, which caused Snaps to jump with surprise. He looked round, and a head peered out at him from behind a row of shelves. It was the gentleman he had already seen that morning. What a coincidence that he should run into him again. The gentleman gathered up the books he had let fall and walked towards the desk. Snaps turned his back to him so as not to be nosey. Presently, the young girl reappeared. Snaps pretended to be looking at the list of plays and films that was hanging to the right of the desk, yet all the time he was keeping a close watch on the man's movements. The books were a complete set of the novels of Charles Dickens. The girl checked them out for him, and then the gentleman left.

Snaps went back to the counter. 'By the way, my name is Snaps,' he said. 'What's yours?'

'I'm Julie.' She handed him the signed docket. Snaps took it and placed it carefully in his shoulder-bag. Then he said: 'It's a funny thing, but I've seen that gentleman twice today already. Who is he?'

'Why, that's Dr Gripp,' Julie answered.

'And is he allowed to do that – take out all those books, I mean?'

'Yes, of course. He's got a special reader's ticket; he can take out as many books as he wants.'

'But don't you miss them? I mean what if someone else comes in looking for the complete works of Dickens?'

'Oh, we've got plenty of those. We simply go down and fetch them from the basement, or else we check around with the other libraries to see who has a set to spare.'

'Through your computer, right?'

'Yes.' Julie was quite good with computers. She pointed to the large computer behind her. 'You see this machine here? Well, this has a link-up with all other libraries in London. We know exactly which books are in each library, who has borrowed them, and all that sort of thing. We also have a link with the British Library, and with libraries outside the city as well, though I don't have the code for those.'

'Gee!' said Snaps. He was becoming really interested. 'Let's say if you wanted to know what books Dr Gripp has borrowed from other libraries, well, that computer could tell you, right?'

'In a flash!' Julie answered.

'Well, let's do it,' said Snaps. 'I'd love to see this thing work.'

'Hey, wait a minute,' Julie objected. 'I'm not supposed to do that sort of thing without a special reason.' Snaps thought for a moment.

'Oh well, if you're not able to work it, then that's OK.'

'I didn't say I wasn't able to work it. I said I can't, except for a special reason.'

'Well, I've got a special reason. I think he's rather sinister. . .' Snaps held a serious expression for a moment, and then a broad smile spread across his face. They both went into hysterics of laughter.

'OK,' said Julie. 'I suppose it wouldn't matter that much.'

She keyed the password into the computer, along with Dr Gripp's name, and his code number. She waited a moment. Almost immediately, a list of the books he had borrowed appeared on the screen.

'Wow!' said Julie. 'Look at that.'

The list was endless. It showed that Dr Gripp had borrowed books from almost every library in London. And not just single books, but entire collections. Snaps read quickly down through the list: *Paradise Lost*, *Gulliver's Travels*, *Shakespeare's Tragedies*, *War and Peace*, *The Adventures of Huckleberry Finn*, *The Adventures of Tom Sawyer*, *The Canterbury Tales*, *Doctor Jekyll and Mister Hyde*, *The Little House on the Prairie*, *Asterix*, *The Complete Paddington*, *Wuthering Heights* . . . The list was endless. At the bottom corner of the screen was written *cont.*, which meant that there was more to come. Julie touched a key, and the entire screen filled up again.

'Gee whizz!' said Snaps. 'Just look at that. Now why would someone need to borrow so many books?'

'I don't know,' said Julie, thoughtfully. 'Maybe he's a professor or something.'

'Or a thief,' Snaps added. 'Tell me, who exactly *is* this Dr Gripp anyway?'

Julie cleared the screen, and requested Dr Gripp's file. Presently the following appeared: 'Dr Samuel Gripp, 29 Ridge Rd., N8 9LJ. Occupation: Variable. Research interests: void.'

'Is that it?' Snaps asked.

'That's it, I'm afraid.'

'Doesn't tell us very much, does it?'

'No, not really. He obviously values his privacy.'

'One last thing,' said Snaps, 'can you give me a printout of those books he's borrowed? I'd like to take a closer look at them.'

'Hey, I'm not supposed to have done even this much.' Julie's voice had lowered. 'I just *can't* give you a print-out. OK?'

'OK,' said Snaps. 'Could you do something else for me then? Could you keep me informed of any further books he borrows?'

'Well, yes . . . I suppose so . . .,' Julie answered doubt-fully.

'Just ring Pilkington's and ask for Snaps Kelly.'

'Sure,' Julie agreed. Then she added: 'But listen. No one must know about this. I've done enough already to get myself fired for good.'

'My lips are sealed!' Snaps said as he headed for the door. 'Bye. And thanks.'

'Bye,' she whispered, and gave him a broad smile.

'Next stop Bloomsbury!' Snaps said to himself as he went back down Euston Road towards the British Library and Museum.

Upstairs, in the Oriental Department of the museum, a special exhibition was being held. Earlier that year, an ancient papyrus had been discovered in Devon by a farmer who was out ploughing his field. Papyrus is the earliest form of paper ever used by man, and this particular one was supposed to be the oldest in the world. Snaps wondered what an ancient piece of paper might look like (not great, as you can imagine), and as it was coming near lunch-time, he decided to go and take a look. The papyrus was in a large display unit upstairs, just past the mummy room.

It wasn't much to look at really, just a thick, dark, dirty, brown piece of funny-looking paper. It had some writing on it which was very hard to make out. Still, people were giving it an awful lot of attention, and who should be there among them but the mysterious Dr Gripp. Funnily enough, Snaps was not that surprised to see him yet again. He was still dressed in the white suit, except on this occasion he was wearing a small yellow rose in the buttonhole of his jacket. He was closely studying the papyrus, as if he had some special interest in it. Then, suddenly, he turned away and hurried down the marble stairs towards the exit. Snaps watched him closely. He had a funny feeling that he would be seeing him again soon . . .

—3—

What's All This About Monkeys?

When Snaps arrived home that evening there was a
police car parked outside his house in Fitzroy Square.
'Oh, no!' he thought. 'What has Grandpa been up to
this time!' Quickly, he rushed upstairs, past the Galaxy
Room, and into the living quarters on the top floor.
Grandpa was sitting cross-legged on the coffee table,
humming to himself with his eyes closed. He was
dressed like Mahatma Gandhi, with a sheet tied round
his waist, and a big medallion around his neck, which
said 'Elvis Lives'. A monster curry was boiling on the
stove. Snaps was surprised to see no policemen anywhere.

'Hey, Grandpa,' he said. 'There's a police car parked
outside.' Grandpa opened one eye. 'I sure hope so,' he
said.

'How did it get there?' Snaps enquired.

'I put it there,' Grandpa answered.

'You don't mean to say . . .' Snaps's mouth fell open

like a drawer. Grandpa opened both eyes. 'Ask no questions,' he said, hopping off the coffee table. He went over to the stove and sniffed the curry. It smelt like old socks or boiled runners. Grandpa made a terrible face. 'Yuk!' he shouted. 'Who made this stuff?' Then he turned to Snaps and said: 'Get your clothes changed, my boy. We're going out to dinner!' He slopped a spoonful of curry on to Fitzroy's dish, and threw the rest of it down the rubbish chute, saucepan, spoon and all. Fitzroy looked at the steaming, smelly curry, and then up at Grandpa. 'You must be joking!' he seemed to say.

Meanwhile, Snaps was tucking into a bowl of exploding cartwheels. Grandpa went into the bedroom, and came out again dressed in his best suit, which wasn't that good really. He grabbed Snaps by the arm.

'Let's go!' he shouted. 'I'm starving. I could eat a small horse.' Snaps had barely time to finish his bowl of *Sugar Snaps* before he was yanked out of the door, down the stairs and into Grandpa's new police car.

The car was a bit slow to start, and a bit rattley under the bonnet, but it was OK once it got going. 'Hold on to your potatoes!' said Grandpa as he put his boot to the floor, and the car zoomed forward like a rocket.

Snaps was not surprised when Grandpa chose one of the best restaurants in London. He brought the car to a sudden stop, and parked it on top of a double yellow line.

'You can't park here,' Snaps objected.

'Of course I can!' answered Grandpa. 'It's a police car, isn't it?'

If the arrival at the restaurant was total confusion,

then the meal itself was pure chaos. Grandpa ordered just about everything, then changed his mind about a hundred times. Having insulted every single dish the chef had to offer, the chef himself was forced to make an appearance to find out what exactly would satisfy Detective G. Kelly of the London Constabulary. When Grandpa saw the size of the chef (a good six and a half feet), he immediately ordered sausages and chips, some toast, and a cup of strong tea, with apple tart and custard for dessert. Snaps asked for some prawns, some salad, and a bowl of exploding cartwheels. Everything had calmed down nicely until the waiter brought the bill. Grandpa read it, frowned grumpily, and then searched in each of his ragged pockets. From the inside pocket of his jacket he took a dead mouse, one that Fitzroy had cornered under the fridge at home, and he slipped it under the piece of uneaten apple tart that lay on his plate.

Grandpa slowly wiped his lips, like an actor finishing a stage meal, and put his napkin down in great satisfaction.

Then, winking at Snaps, he stood up and let out a tremendous roar: '*Ahhhhhhhh.*' Everyone looked round. The waiter came over promptly.

'Is there something the matter, sir?' he asked.

Grandpa held up the dead mouse and everyone in the restaurant said: '*Ohhhhhhhhhhhh.*' Then Grandpa started telling the waiter that he had never been more embarrassed in his entire life, what was the meaning of this mouse, and all that sort of stuff. He also said that when he went back to the police station he would be filing a special report on the matter, and that the restaurant owner would be lucky to get away with a hefty fine for serving dangerous food. Grandpa cleaned off the mouse and put it back into his pocket 'for evidence', as he said. Snaps really pitied the poor waiter – he looked so down in the mouth and a little blue. Snaps thought that Grandpa had laid it on a bit thick, but then, that was the way he always did things. There were no half measures with Grandpa. The waiter took the bill and tore it in half, hoping that he could improve matters. But no! Grandpa kept on raving and ranting about how hard policemen have to work, and how it's a shame that you can't get a decent meal on your one night off without someone trying to make you eat cooked mouse. He demanded a glass of wine 'to soothe his nerves', and when the waiter poured him a glass, Grandpa took the entire bottle. 'Ha-Ha!' he said. 'You fell for that one didn't you? It's an old police trick, you know. Now I've got your fingerprints as well!' And sticking the bottle into his raggy pocket he strolled out of the door.

Snaps was glad to get outside away from all the confusion. His one fear was that the six-and-a-half-foot chef might reappear to give Grandpa an awful thumping, so he was glad when they got safely into the police car and zoomed off.

'Where to, my lad?' said Grandpa as he took a swig from the bottle of wine. Snaps thought for a moment. He had had enough excitement for one night, of that he was sure.

'There's an address I want to check out. 29 Ridge Road. It's in the Hampstead direction. Do you think we could go there to take a look? I've a feeling it might be important.'

'Ten-four!' answered Grandpa, putting his boot to the floor. The police car was a rocket again.

Grandpa's driving was atrocious, but, amazingly, he had never had an accident in his life. And he had driven every sort of vehicle you could mention, everything from a penny-farthing bicycle to a flying-carpet.

Funnily enough, Snaps had not yet seen him on the huge motorbike which he kept beside the bed, and when he asked Grandpa about it, he said: 'I'm still working on it.'

Soon they arrived at Hampstead, and using his A to Z of London, Snaps directed Grandpa to Ridge Road. Number 29 was half-way down on the left.

'Let's go quietly,' said Snaps, 'so as not to attract attention.'

'Good idea,' said Grandpa as he kabroomed down the road and stopped with a screech of brakes outside number 29. It was coming on for twilight, and Ridge Road was deserted.

'Seems empty,' said Snaps, looking at the unlit and uncurtained windows of Dr Gripp's house.

'I should think so,' said Grandpa, pointing to a sign which said: *Residence for Sale or Rent. Ring 902820.*

'So you've come about the monkeys, right?' A woman had stuck her head in the window of the police car. Grandpa jumped.

'Who are you?' he asked.

'I'm the responsible citizen who rang you about that Griffy chap, or whatever his name is. Oh, it was really terrible. I mean you can't have people keeping dozens of wild animals in a residential area like this. It just isn't right, as I was saying to my George the other day. George, I said, it just isn't right, and he said no dear, it isn't.'

'Hang on a minute,' said Snaps. 'Slow down a bit. What's all this about monkeys?'

'Dozens of 'em there were. All kept in cages stacked up in the garden, and some inside the house as well. Oh, the noisy chatter all day long and at night as well. And nasty little devils they were too, not nice monkeys like the ones in the zoo, as I was saying to my George the other day, and he said no dear, the ones in the zoo are much nicer. Well, we just had to complain, because this is a nice area you know. Anyways, he just packed up and left. He took away all his monkeys and cages and things in a big lorry and just left. Last week it was, and good riddance I say. So, you've had a trip up here for nothing. You chaps really are policemen, aren't you?'

Grandpa reached for his badge and opened it with an expert flick.

'Plain-clothes,' he said, 'just like on telly.'

The woman looked at Snaps.

'Isn't that one a little young?' she said.

'Special witness in a difficult case,' said Grandpa. 'His information could lead us to the stolen monkeys.'

'*Stolen* monkeys! You mean to say those monkeys were *stolen*?'

''Fraid so,' said Grandpa with a sigh.

'But why did you let him get away then when you knew he was here?'

'It's all part of the plan, ma'am. We want the stolen monkeys to lead us to the stolen parrots.'

'Stolen parrots! You mean there are stolen parrots as well!'

'Yes, ma'am. We simply must find the stolen parrots. They're the only ones who can tell us where the missing elephant is.'

'Missing elephant! My goodness,' said the woman.

'Well, we'd better be going,' said Grandpa. 'By the way, do you have any idea where this chap has moved to?'

'No, I'm afraid I don't. And I was saying to my George just the other . . .'

'OK, ma'am, thank you for your help. And don't forget, if you see any stray elephants acting suspiciously, be a good citizen and contact the police immediately. OK?'

'I will. I really will,' answered the woman; and with that she went running down the footpath shouting 'George . . . George . . . just wait till you hear this . . .' Grandpa did an expert U-turn on the road and, his elbow resting casually on the window, they headed back towards the city, under the blood-red twilight sky.

When they reached home, Fitzroy was waiting patiently on the doorstep. Grandpa threw him the dead mouse (which now tasted a little of peppermints from Grandpa's pocket) and Fitzroy swallowed it with a gulp. Upstairs, Grandpa changed into his astronomer's clothes and went out on the roof to explore the sky.

'Isn't it the wrong time of year for star-gazing?' Snaps asked, as Grandpa headed up through the ceiling. 'I mean, wouldn't winter-time be much better?'

'Who's star-gazing?' said Grandpa rather grumpily.

'Don't tell me you're still looking for UFOs?'

'Of course not!'

'Well, what then?'

'Unicorns!' said Grandpa, and he scrambled up the ladder and out on to the roof.

'Oh boy!' Snaps said to himself as he flopped into an armchair and turned on the telly.

The late film was half over but he watched it anyway. It was called *Gnaws*, and it was about a huge rat which had escaped from a professor's laboratory and that went around the city chewing up people, and generally making a nuisance of himself. Snaps yawned and then dozed off in the comfortable armchair. When he woke up it was almost midnight. The late news was over and Open University was just about to start. He stretched himself and got up to head for bed. Just as he was about to turn off the telly he heard the compère announce: '. . . and here to present some interesting facts about the brown monkeys of Borneo is the distinguished zoologist Dr Samuel Gripp.'

Snaps called out for Grandpa who came down off the roof wondering what all the excitement was about. They both stood gazing at the person on the TV screen.

'Aha!' said Grandpa. 'So he's a zoologist. That accounts for the monkeys.'

'Yes. But what about all the library books,' said Snaps. 'How do you account for those?'

Grandpa shrugged. He poured out a glass of wine for himself, and a saucerful for Fitzroy.

'I don't know,' Grandpa said. 'Maybe he just gets tired of all the monkey business?'

'I wonder . . .' Snaps said, thoughtfully. 'There has to be an explanation. There just has to be. I wonder what it is . . .'

−4−

More Monkey Business

When Snaps arrived at Fleet Street the next morning
there was a surprise in store for him. Three police cars
(real ones) were pulled up outside Mr Webster's stamp
shop, and a few people had gathered outside, even
though it was still quite early. The shop itself was open,
and a police-officer was questioning Mr Webster, who
was sitting on a chair with his face in his hands. During
the night someone had broken in and stolen his priceless
stamp collection. Poor Mr Webster. He was heart-
broken. 'My precious stamps,' he kept saying. 'My
children. All gone, taken from me, vanished into thin
air . . .' In the background, other policemen were rummaging around looking for clues.

'Please tell me again what happened,' the police-
officer said to Mr Webster, and Mr Webster started his
story all over again: how he had locked his shop,
checked all the shutters and the security doors before
retiring upstairs.

48

'But don't you lock it away,' said the smart police-officer, 'your priceless collection, I mean?'

Mr Webster looked very solemn. He took his hands from his face, and looked the policeman straight in the eye.

'For forty years I've been a stamp merchant on Fleet Street,' he said. 'So too were my father and grandfather before me, and in all that time nothing like this has ever happened. Stamps are to be looked at, loved, and enjoyed, not locked away in some lonely place. Often at night, when I couldn't sleep, I'd sneak down here to look at my priceless treasures – my children, I'd call them – and the sight of them would calm my restless heart.' Mr Webster looked away into the distance. He seemed to be remembering a time that had vanished for ever. 'Sometimes, in the old days, I'd never lock the shop at all. I'd just pull down the blind on the door and turn around the sign that said *Closed*. And I could go to bed and sleep quite happy. Now this place is like a fortress, with all the locked doors and barred windows. And what good are they after all?'

The policeman remained silent for a moment. Then he asked: 'Do you leave anything unlocked?'

'Just a small window for ventilation. It gets very stuffy in here in summer, you know.' Mr Webster pointed to a tiny window high up near the ceiling at the back of the shop. Then he added: 'A cat could hardly fit in there. I don't know how the thief got in. I really don't . . .'

'Was anything disturbed?'

'Absolutely nothing. The whole affair is a mystery.'

'And you heard no suspicious sounds from upstairs?'

'No.'

The policeman thought for a moment.

'Do many people visit your shop?' he asked.

'I'm not quite sure,' said Mr Webster. 'Hundreds each day, I suppose . . .'

'Well, perhaps someone hid in your shop overnight, stole the stamp collection, and then slipped out when you opened up this morning.' The police-officer spoke with the authority of a person who suddenly knew all the answers.

'I suppose so,' said Mr Webster. 'But I think that's unlikely.'

'But not impossible,' said the police-officer. 'Take a look around you. This is a very old shop, with lots of passageways, nooks and corners. A thief could have hidden just about anywhere without being noticed. It's quite possible that's exactly what happened.'

'You mean someone was here all night without my knowing about it?' said Mr Webster. The police-officer nodded.

'No, I can't believe that could actually happen,' continued Mr Webster. 'These things only happen on television. Who would really do such a thing? All the visitors to my shop are decent people. None of them would do such a terrible thing.'

The police-officer sighed.

'Times have changed, Mr Webster,' he said. 'Thieves don't go round wearing striped pullovers and carrying sacks that say *Swag*. No, they're much more cunning these days. And sometimes it's the simplest plan that works the best. Like hiding in your shop, for example. What's the best way to get into a place that's a fortress by night? Simply walk in during the day and hide there until the next morning.'

While the police-officer and Mr Webster continued their discussion, Snaps went through to the back of the shop, out of the door and into the yard. Two younger policemen were inspecting the outside, but so far they had found nothing of interest. High above them was the tiny open window which Mr Webster had pointed out, but it was much too small for anyone to have climbed through, even if they did manage to climb over the huge rear wall.

'Might as well search these,' said one of the young policemen pointing at the three large rubbish bins in Mr Webster's backyard. But alas, they were filled only with old envelopes, paper clippings, shredded correspondence, and the butts of Mr Webster's cigars. No, the thief certainly didn't get in the back way, so it looked like the hidden-visitor-theory might, indeed, be true.

Just then, a small item on the ground caught Snaps's eye. He would not have noticed it at all if the young policeman hadn't moved Mr Webster's dustbins to one side. It was a small yellow rose. It was flattened and dirty, but a yellow rose nonetheless. Snaps picked it up and looked at it carefully.

'What have you got there?' asked one of the young policemen.

'Oh, it's nothing,' said Snaps. 'Just an old flower. I thought it was something special.' The young policeman looked at it.

'Hmmm,' he said. 'I see. Probably came from over there, from Mr Jaeger's, the florist.'

Snaps looked across in the direction of the policeman's gaze. Behind them was the yard of Mr Jaeger the florist, and his dustbins were filled up with withered yellow roses.

'Yes, I suppose so,' said Snaps. All the same, he wasn't really sure.

Snaps went back into Mr Webster's shop. Poor Mr Webster was still sitting with his face in his hands.

'My precious stamps,' he kept saying. 'My children. All gone, taken from me, vanished into thin air . . .'

All that morning in Pilkington Ltd, there was great regret at Mr Webster's misfortune. Agnes said it was a terrible thing to happen, he was such a nice man. Mr Pilkington told them all to be on their guard against shady-looking characters, and he instructed Iain to inspect the store-room every evening to check that no one was hiding there. Iain was delighted. He asked Mr Pilkington should he go now and check for burglars just in case someone was hiding back there (really, he was dying for a cigarette). But Mr Pilkington said no, they were probably quite safe for the moment. Bill Heap said he didn't know what all the excitement was about. Just imagine, an old battered stamp collection creating such a fuss. Mr Henry glared across at him. 'Some people have no respect,' he mumbled to himself, and he glared across at Bill Heap yet again.

As the morning wore on, Snaps went about his usual chores of checking the lists, sorting the mail, running errands and getting deliveries ready. It was coming on for eleven-thirty. Bill Heap had left a long time ago, and the postman still hadn't arrived.

'OK,' said Mr Pilkington. 'I suppose you'd better get going. The postman is pretty late this morning, though I can't imagine why.'

Snaps loaded up the side saddles of his moped and prepared to head off on his daily rounds. Just as he was about to leave, he saw Miss Creef trotting along the footpath. She was in her usual last-minute hurry.

'Oh dear! Oh dear! Oh dear!' she said. 'There was such a fuss at Russell Street that I nearly didn't get through at all!' She was carrying a bag that said Harrods of London, and that was filled with all sorts of parcels wrapped up in Christmas paper. Snaps looked at the parcels and then at Miss Creef. 'Good grief! Isn't it a little early for Christmas shopping?' he said. Miss Creef clutched the parcels towards her, and searched in her small head for something to say.

'Why of course it is,' she said at last. 'It's just that Mildred is having some friends over from Australia, and the Australians always celebrate Christmas during the summer, you know. So we thought we'd surprise them with a few presents. We must be nice to our foreign friends, now mustn't we. Now, I think I'd better toddle along. Good morning, Master Snaps.'

'More like good afternoon,' Snaps said to himself as he put on his helmet.

'And by the way,' Miss Creef added, 'if you have any deliveries for the British Museum or Library, don't waste your time going over there. It's closed.'

'Closed?' Snaps repeated. 'Now why would it be closed?'

'Why, because of the robbery, of course. Haven't you listened to the news this morning? Something was stolen from the museum last night. Some sort of pre-historic paper, or something like that. First time it's ever happened. It's been on telly all morning . . . Well, I'd better be going. Toodle-doo. Oh, Master Snaps, if you're going past Buck and Company would you check whether they have any Christmas trees in yet?'

Snaps got off his bike and ran the short distance down the road to Ladbroke's betting shop.

'Hey kid! You're not supposed to be in here!' a man shouted from behind a counter.

'Sorry,' said Snaps. 'This is an emergency,' and he reached up to change the channel on the television. The racehorses and little jockeys flickered out, and a special report from Russell Street appeared.

'And can you tell us anything about your plans to recover the missing papyrus?' a reporter was asking a serious-looking gentleman with a shiny head who had just got out of a big car and was squeezing through the crowds of people outside the huge black railings.

'I'm afraid I have no comment at the moment,' the man was saying with a sort of plastic smile on his worried face. 'No comment at all at the moment.' The reporter then turned to face the TV camera and said: 'We are here in front of the gates of the British Museum. As you are no doubt aware of by now, the famous Devon papyrus has mysteriously disappeared from its stand in the exhibition hall where it was on display. Forensic experts are presently examining the site of the "crime", if indeed this *is* a crime rather than a humorous prank. A preliminary enquiry has failed to reveal how anyone might have entered and escaped from this well-secured building, or how someone could have managed to remove the papyrus without setting off the sophisticated alarm-system. This event is the first of its kind in Britain for some time . . .'

'What about Mr Webster's stamp collection?' asked Snaps.

The reporter looked up in astonishment and stared out of the screen at Snaps.

'Oh yes,' the reporter continued. 'We have just heard that a stamp-dealer in Fleet Street ... a certain Mr Weller ...'

'Webster,' said Snaps.

'Mr Webster, I think that is ...' continued the reporter, 'has reported the theft of a precious collection of stamps. Police are continuing their enquiries into both these incidents, but they feel that the missing articles are already out of the country, and are probably in Japan ...'

'Japan?' asked Snaps. 'Why Japan?'

'I'm not quite sure why,' said the reporter. 'I don't write this stuff, you know. I just read it ... And with that I'll hand you back to the studio.'

Snaps switched channels, and galloping racehorses appeared again.

'This is terrible,' said Snaps.

'Sure is,' said the man behind the counter. 'I was hoping number seven would win, but he's way behind.'

All that day Snaps was barely able to concentrate on his work. His mind was filled with questions, theories and possibilities. How had two priceless treasures disappeared in the same night? To steal *one* would have been an achievement; to steal both was almost unbelievable! Unless, of course, the whole thing was a mere coincidence, and both crimes were done by different people. Yet, the more he thought about the matter, the more he believed that Dr Gripp was somehow mixed up in these mysterious events ...

— 5 —

A Trail of Missing Paper

For a few days there was nothing but talk about the stolen treasures. Every major newspaper in the world carried reports, and Mr Webster's picture appeared on the front page of *The Times*. At street corners, in the tube-stations, and on the buses, people were chatting to each other saying how terrible it was, imagine such a thing happening, in England of all places, and all that sort of thing. As the weekend approached there was less talk, and the frenzy died down a bit. By the middle of the next week there was even less, and soon there was none at all. The British Museum reopened with the public display of a skeleton they kept for emergencies. He was supposed to be the oldest skeleton in existence. He had a big grin on him and seemed to enjoy making an exhibition of himself. Mr Webster had not closed his shop at all, saying that he closed only at Christmas, Easter, Bank Holidays and on the Queen's birthday, and that he didn't see why he should let a low criminal interrupt a routine he had been practising for years. But really, he was a sorry sight as he removed his shutters every morning, saying hello to everybody and trying to be cheerful. He had got Mr Pilkington to print thousands of leaflets asking for information leading to the recovery of his stamps, and offering a reward. Snaps and Mr Henry volunteered to deliver these leaflets to houses, shops, factories, theatres and cinemas; they put some on the windscreens of cars, but so far no information had been received. True, the police were continuing their enquiries behind the scenes, but absolutely no clues were discovered. At the moment, Mr Webster had a big wreath in his shop window, the type that people carry at funerals. He said that there would be a wreath of flowers in his window every day, until such time as his stamps were recovered.

It was now approaching the middle of July. London got so hot it sizzled. Each evening after the news, the brown-faced and red-nosed weatherman said it was the hottest summer on record, with temperatures soaring into the nineties. One evening he said that tomorrow would be so hot that you could probably fry an egg on the pavement. So the next morning, Grandpa decided he'd try it. Snaps was digging into his third bowl of *Sugar Snaps*, and Fitzroy was lapping up his third saucer of milk as Grandpa headed downstairs carrying two eggs and a lump of butter. He also took the frying-pan just in case any weirdos bothered him. He chose the sunniest bit of pavement in Fitzroy Square and buttered it nicely before cracking the two eggs. Then he waited for them to fry.

'What's going on?' one passer-by whispered to

another at a bus-stop. 'I'm not quite sure,' the other answered. 'I think it's some sort of modern art.' But Grandpa (who had eyes like an eagle and ears like Prince Charles) spun round and said: 'It might be art to you, mate, but it's my breakfast!' The eggs, of course, didn't fry. They just lay there like big sad eyes on the footpath. One small man with a briefcase nearly stepped on them as he was running for a taxi. Grandpa ran after him and made a swipe at his head with the frying-pan. Luckily, he missed. When he went back to his spot on the footpath, a dog was sniffing at his eggs. Grandpa made another swipe with his frying-pan and this time he didn't miss.

In the end, Grandpa gave up, and went across to Manuel's for a cup of coffee and a sandwich. 'Don't believe everything you hear on television,' he said to Manuel as he walked wearily through the door. Manuel looked at him and said bemusedly: 'Eh?' As for the two eggs, they just lay there all morning, and people avoided them as best they could. But then Ms Whetstone, who wasn't looking where she was going, came out of her apartment and walked right on top of them. Now, you know what happens when you step on something slippery that you didn't see. You suddenly fall down, and that's just what happened to Ms Whetstone. She fell right down and banged her head on the silver telegraph pole. Later, when she was having a plaster put on her forehead, the doctor asked her what she had slipped on, and Ms Whetstone said that she wasn't quite sure, but that it looked like some sort of slippery goo.

Life for Snaps was as busy as usual. Every morning he

headed off for Pilkington's where he went through his usual routine.

One morning, as he was about to depart on his rounds, Mr Pilkington shouted to him: 'Hey, Snaps. Telephone.'

Snaps went over and picked up the receiver. It was Julie. Snaps was delighted. He hadn't heard from her for quite some time. She had been away for a short holiday, staying with her grandmother in Cornwall.

'Hi, Julie,' Snaps said. 'It's great to hear from you again!' His voice was high-pitched and excited. They spoke for a while about Julie's holiday, about the lovely weather and the lovely scenery in Cornwall. Then Snaps asked if there was any further news about Dr Gripp. Unfortunately, nothing new had developed. He had not borrowed any more books from any London library. But he had not returned any either.

'That doesn't surprise me,' said Snaps. 'I think he's gone on to bigger and better things.'

'How do you mean?' asked Julie, slightly puzzled. 'What's all this interest in Dr Gripp for anyway?'

'What have a book, a stamp collection, and an ancient papyrus all got in common?' Snaps asked.

'If you mean to suggest their value, well forget it,' said Julie. 'Those library books aren't really that valuable, you know. They're just library books, that's all. And if you're suggesting that Dr Gripp had something to do with the stamp and paper affairs, well that's the most preposterous thing I ever heard. Not everyone who borrows books from a library is a thief. Don't you agree?'

'I don't know what to think, really,' said Snaps. Then he added: 'Why don't we meet each other for lunch and talk about the entire affair?'

'Yes, that's a great idea,' said Julie. 'I'd like that.'

'By the way, have you found any current address for Dr Gripp?'

'I haven't been able to find an address anywhere. He's obviously a man who values his privacy.'

'A bit curious, don't you think?' said Snaps.

Snaps and Julie met for lunch at one o'clock, and they went across to the small shaded park in Woburn Square. As they walked through the gates of the park, a small man was fixing a poster to the railings. The poster said: *Come and See Raymond's Roadshow – The Greatest Show on Earth. Last Day Today*. Raymond's Roadshow was a small broken-down circus that Snaps had often passed on his trips through the city.

Snaps and Julie sat under a huge tree, whose wide spreading branches almost touched the ground.

'Do you really think Dr Gripp is mixed up in the recent robberies?' Julie asked, as she uncapped a small carton of yoghurt. Snaps looked around and then nodded rather seriously. 'But how? I mean how did he do them? The police found no clues, absolutely nothing, not even a fingerprint. Just how did he do it, then? Can he walk through walls, or locked doors, or climb through miniature windows?'

'Course not,' said Snaps as he helped himself to some more lunch-time cereal.

'Well, what's the answer then?'

Snaps stood up, grabbed one of the low-hanging branches, and swung from it by his legs. Then he ran in a circle on his hands and knees, making a funny *uh–uh–uh* sound. Julie laughed and spluttered yoghurt over her T-shirt.

'What's that supposed to be?' she asked.

'Monkeys,' said Snaps, and he sat down beside her again.

'Monkeys?' asked Julie, rather puzzled.

'Yes, monkeys. That's how he did those robberies. He used trained monkeys. He used them to climb through the tiny window in Mr Webster's shop, and to climb into the museum. Yes, I'm sure of it. The stamp affair was rather a simple job, I guess. The museum affair was rather a different matter, because of the alarm and things. But by climbing down from somewhere above the display unit, rather than by scampering across the floor towards it, the alarm would probably not have been activated at all. Yes, I'm quite sure of it . . .'

Julie looked rather grave as she listened to Snaps's theory on Dr Gripp. Then she took a small piece of rolled up paper from her pocket.

'What's that?' Snaps asked with interest.

'It's probably nothing important. But after I had been talking to you this morning I decided to look up the library catalogue to see if Dr Gripp had ever written anything himself, perhaps a book or an article for a magazine or something. In fact, he wrote a rather obscure book which was published a long time ago. I wrote down the title of it on this.'

She handed Snaps the piece of paper which said: *Parasites of the Lesser Mongolian Monkey* by Samuel Gripp (Bombay 1967).

'It figures,' said Snaps. 'Monkeys in the backyard, monkeys in the stamp shop and in the museum, monkeys on TV, and now monkeys in the library.'

'I doubt if that book was ever top of the bestsellers' list,' Julie said with a laugh. 'Still, maybe there's something to your monkey theory after all.'

61

'OK,' said Snaps, 'we'd better get a move on if we're to get back to work on time.'

'Hang on a minute,' Julie said. 'I've something else for you.' She handed Snaps a small envelope. He opened it. Inside there was a small piece of coral on a little silver chain.

'I made it myself,' said Julie rather shyly. 'While I was on the beach.' Then she took it from Snaps's hands and put it round his neck. Snaps felt all tingly and wobbly at the knees. He thought he must be falling in love. He hoped he wasn't, because he had first to solve a lot of problems before he had time for girls. Just like detectives on TV: they never fell in love until just before the end of the programme when all the criminals were caught, and all the mysteries were tided up . . .

Snaps need not have worried about falling in love. For the next few days he had plenty of other things to think about. In the first place, it was the busy time for the printing trade, and Pilkington's was simply bursting with business. Then there was the routine trouble with Grandpa, who kept getting up to his usual tricks. He had suddenly decided that he was getting too old for climbing stairs, so he had a new lift installed, and he nearly demolished half the building in the process. When Snaps came home from Pilkington's one evening, all the stairs had been removed, and a huge square hole had been bored through all the ceilings right up to the top floor. When Snaps looked up, he saw Grandpa's grey wrinkled head peering down at him from far above. Ms Whetstone just happened to pass by the front door, and she asked Snaps: 'What's the old devil up to now?' When she caught a glimpse of the mess inside, she hurried off shaking her head and muttering: 'He should have been locked up years ago.'

It took three days to install the new lift, and in the mean time Snaps and Grandpa used a rope ladder to get up and down. Grandpa looked like an ancient mariner climbing up the rigging of a ship as his skinny legs and arms scambled up and down the rope ladder. In the end the lift was finished and it worked like magic. Snaps thought it was just about worth the trouble after all.

There were other events, too, that attracted Snaps's attention. Two important scrolls disappeared from the University in Cambridge, and a poem with William Shakespeare's signature on it went missing from Oxford. Once again, the TV cameras zoomed in, and the newspapers went ape with photos, interviews and reports. Within another few days, important water-colour paintings were found to be missing from Christie's collection in Bristol, as well as a paper hat that had once been worn by Winston Churchill at a Christmas party. A little woman in Brighton reported the disappearance of her pension book, but this was later found to have fallen down behind the settee. Finally, a consignment of Indian tea-bags was stolen from a ship at London docks, but police were not sure whether this had any connection with the other robberies. In any case, it looked as if a trail of missing paper was slowly and surely spreading all over England . . .

-6-

Dark Clouds Above the Rain

'*Shall I Die, Shall I Fly,*' Snaps said.

'Shall I which, shall I what?' asked Grandpa.

'*Shall I Die, Shall I Fly,*' Snaps repeated. 'That's the title of the missing poem by William Shakespeare. Imagine, it was just discovered a short time ago, and now it's missing already.'

'Did they have aeroplanes in those days?' asked Grandpa. 'Gee, I never knew they had aeroplanes in those days.'

Snaps and Grandpa were outside on the roof of the building. The sky had darkened, and veiled itself for evening. Above them were black thunder-clouds that they could almost touch; all around them the heat was sweltering. There was a sudden rumble in the distance, and a visible flash.

'We're going to have thunder,' said Snaps, 'and buckets of rain.'

Grandpa wasn't listening. He was looking through

his telescope at a Boeing 747 heading, with lights twinkling, towards Heathrow.

'You wouldn't catch me up in one of those things,' he muttered. Then he turned round and said to Fitzroy: 'Aren't you going out this evening, cat?'

Fitzroy looked up at the dark thunder-clouds and then up at Grandpa. 'Are you kidding?' he seemed to say.

'I've figured out how he does it,' said Snaps. 'Or at least I think so. Only I can't figure out how everything ties in . . . Grandpa, are you listening to me?'

'Why, of course not,' said Grandpa. He had picked out a white-clad figure standing in a doorway a few streets away. Snaps thought he felt a drop of rain.

'Better take your telescope inside, Grandpa,' he said. 'The heavens are going to open.'

Snaps went back into the living-room where Fitzroy was sitting upright on a chair watching a cat-food advertisement on TV. Grandpa gathered up his telescope with a clatter, and hurried down through the trapdoor into the room below. Instead of turning into the living-room, he went straight ahead into the lift.

'Hey! Where are you going?' Snaps called out.

'Police business!' Grandpa answered. 'Mind the office till I get back.' And he disappeared behind the sliding doors, with the telescope on his shoulder. Once outside, he placed the telescope on the back seat of the police car, sat in the front, and started up the engine. He was just in time, too, for just then the heavens opened and a huge downpour hit the streets of London.

Grandpa drove down the street at high speed. The rain was hopping like golf balls off the bonnet of the

65

car. He hoped he wasn't too late. He came to a sudden stop behind a row of taxis and, taking the telescope with him, he headed for the last one in the line. He opened the boot of the taxi and packed the telescope awkwardly inside. Then he yanked the driver out into the rain. 'Sorry mate,' he said, flashing his police badge. 'Important business to attend to.' And with that, he zoomed off leaving the unfortunate taxi-driver standing sodden and bemused on the pavement.

Grandpa took the corner on two wheels almost, but once he was on the next street, he slowed to a normal speed again. He felt sure his plan would work, unless he was already too late. He cruised slowly down the street, watching closely for a person dressed in a white suit. He reckoned he had seen him somewhere along here, unless, of course, he had got his calculations wrong . . . But just then, sure enough, a white-clad figure suddenly appeared from a doorway, holding a wet newspaper over his head and waving excitedly. It was Dr Gripp. Grandpa grinned to himself, and came to an expert stop beside the kerb. Dr Gripp got in, and flicked some drops of rain from his beautiful suit.

'Where to, gov?' said Grandpa.

'Hadley Chase, Greenwich,' said Dr Gripp. 'You know where that is?'

'Sure do, gov,' said Grandpa, as he headed off. But, of course, Grandpa didn't know where Hadley Chase was. He had only been to Greenwich once in his life. So naturally, on this occasion, he got hopelessly lost. Dr Gripp kept asking: 'Are you sure you know where you're going?' And Grandpa kept assuring him that he did. Eventually, after about two hours and numerous wrong turns as well as trips down one-way streets, Dr

Gripp said: 'Perhaps if you'd allow me to direct you . . .' But Grandpa refused any assistance. He said he was perfectly capable of finding his way to Greenwich, which was, after all, just on the outskirts of London and not in Timbuctoo. Still, he said he'd be grateful if Dr Gripp would point out the line of longitude should he happen to spot it. Then Grandpa thought of the clever idea of following a bus marked 'Greenwich'. But, unfortunately, the one he picked happened to be heading back to London for repairs. So the search for Greenwich had to start all over again. Then Grandpa decided to follow the line of the river Thames (which he should have done right at the start) and at last they arrived at their destination. A very weary Dr Gripp directed Grandpa to Hadley Chase.

'You can drop me here, thank you,' he said, pointing to a tall doorway in the wall that surrounded his house. Then, having paid the fare (which was almost a small fortune) he quickly went inside.

Grandpa drove off as if towards London, but almost immediately he doubled back. Dr Gripp's house looked like Fort Knox. The wall completely encircled it, and it was impossible to get even a glimpse inside. The river came right up to the west-side wall. The whole place was like a fortress, impregnable, or at least so it appeared. By the looks of it, his garden seemed huge, and Grandpa reckoned that Dr Gripp was a very wealthy man.

Grandpa remembered that they had passed over a rather steep hill on their descent into Greenwich so he drove off in that direction. A man in a bowler hat waved frantically in the rain and shouted, 'Taxi!' Grandpa swerved smartly into a puddle and splattered the gentleman's suit with dirty, muddy water. Once he had reached the top of the steep hill, Grandpa took his telescope and pointed it in the direction of Dr Gripp's house. He carefully scanned the horizon until it came into view.

The house was really a mansion, and the gardens were gorgeous and huge. Yet apart from its great size, there seemed to be nothing odd about the place. Suddenly, a light went on and Dr Gripp appeared at a window. He seemed to be talking to someone else who was in the room, but Grandpa couldn't see who it was. After a few minutes, the light in the room went off again, and the building was enveloped in the darkness of the gathering dusk. Grandpa sighed. Oh well, at least he had found where the Gripp chap lived, and Snaps would be glad of that. Before putting away the telescope, he scanned the gardens again; and there in a dark corner of the gravel driveway, partially obscured by a huge limousine, was a colourful vehicle that looked like a circus lorry. On the side of it, he could just about make out the words: *Raymond's Roadshow – The Greatest Show on Earth*.

'Wot you looking for, mate?' a voice said from behind him.

'Nothing,' said Grandpa. 'I've just found it!' Then he folded his telescope and headed back for London.

− 7 −

There's More to This Than Meets the Eye . . .

'Yes. It figures. Just as I thought. He *was* using monkeys to carry out all those robberies. Still, it's quite a brilliant cover, you must admit. I mean, what better way to transport a pack of trained thieving monkeys than to use the least suspect method of all – a travelling circus!'

Snaps and Grandpa were talking over supper, and were looking at a poster for Raymond's Roadshow.

'And to think that these posters were hanging all over London right under our noses all the time!' Snaps gave a little incredulous laugh.

'Just look here,' he continued. 'Each of the places visited by the circus over the past few weeks was also the site of a major robbery: first London, then Cambridge, Oxford and Bristol. And St Davids is next on the list. Raymond's Roadshow is scheduled to visit there this weekend. Wow! I can't believe we've discovered this! It's just unbelievable!'

'What's all this *we* stuff,' Grandpa objected. 'It was *my* brilliance that finally broke the case, wasn't it?'

'Sure, Grandpa,' Snaps said. 'You were just fantastic. And so quick-thinking. But I've a feeling that this case is far from over yet . . .'

'Where's this place St Davids, anyway?' Grandpa asked.

'It's in Wales,' Snaps answered, as he poured himself another bowl of *Sugar Snaps*. 'It's the smallest city in the world, a place of immense historical importance. It's also just the sort of place that would attract Dr Gripp and his phoney circus. Now, I wonder what exactly is of interest to him in St Davids? Hang on a minute . . .'

Snaps reached for the evening paper and turned to the pages of advertisements for various events. Almost immediately, he found what he wanted, and gave a long low whistle.

'Listen to this, Grandpa,' he said. '*Unique first edition of the collected works of Beatrix Potter will go on display at Dickson's auctioneering premises in St Davids, Dyfed, from Saturday next. These beautiful children's books, each of which carries the author's signature, will be auctioned the following Wednesday. The collection is expected to fetch at least one million pounds.* Wow, a cool million! This guy really likes to go for the big ones, you'll have to admit that! But he's not going to get away with it this time, because we're going to be there to catch him red-handed, or should I say red-pawed!'

Grandpa looked up from his bowl of soup.

'What are you talking about? Who's going to be where?' he asked.

'We're going to St Davids to welcome Dr Gripp. It's so simple. We'll use the plan that the police thought Dr

Gripp used in Mr Webster's shop, only we now know that he didn't. We'll go to have a look at the books and then when nobody's looking we'll hide somewhere inside there for the night and catch the thieves in the act.'

'Hey, wait a minute,' said Grandpa. 'That's the craziest plan I ever heard. In the first place, what makes you so sure that it's a set of books that's of interest to Dr Gripp. I'm sure St Davids must have plenty of antique shops with lots of treasures stored. Things like priceless stones, or jewellery, or . . .'

'No! No! You don't understand,' Snaps interrupted. 'All of the items stolen so far were priceless, that's true. But they've also all been made of paper. First, Mr Webster's stamps, then the museum papyrus, then the ancient scrolls and the poem and the . . .'

'OK, OK. I see your point,' said Grandpa. 'So this guy is obviously a collector who specializes in paper stuff, right?' Snaps nodded. 'And you want us to put a stop to all his shenanigans, right?' Snaps nodded again. 'Hmm,' said Grandpa and his eyes began to twinkle like splintered glass.

He got up suddenly, and disappeared into his bedroom. Soon he came back out carrying a net, a plastic banana, and dressed in a monkey-suit. Snaps looked at him in disbelief.

'The net and banana are probably a good idea, but really, do you have to wear the suit?'

Grandpa took off the monkey's head.

'Why, of course,' said Grandpa. 'For camouflage! I can do monkey sounds as well.' He took a deep breath, held it for a moment, and then let out a screech that sounded like a poisoned dodo bird. Fitzroy leapt from

71

the chair where he had been curled up asleep, and stood with his back arched, waiting to spring at the first thing that moved.

'OK, Grandpa,' Snaps said with a sigh. 'We'll talk about it tomorrow. Come on, let's get to bed. I've got to get up early in the morning.' He took up the evening paper. 'By the way,' he said to Grandpa, who was struggling out of his monkey-suit, 'have you seen this?'

Snaps pointed to an article that said *Forged Banknotes Circulating in London.* Grandpa looked at the headline, and then whipped from his pocket a banknote that Dr Gripp has given him earlier that evening. He looked at it closely, bit it, and held it up to the light.

'This one seems OK, anyway,' he said with a sigh of relief. Then he read down through the rest of the newspaper article. It described how someone had bad-fingered the banks with phoney money. The banknotes were perfect in every way, right down to the metal strip; however, the paper used to make them was obviously of a very poor quality, because it wrinkled, crumbled and disintegrated after only a short time. The banks, of course, did not discover this until it was too late. They did not, however, feel that there was any need for panic as the forger would be caught quite soon.

'Caught quite soon,' Grandpa said to himself. 'I wouldn't hold my breath if I were you, mate!' He tossed the paper from him, and Snaps picked it up and put it tidily away. 'Really, the world has gone to the dogs! First, funny monkeys, and now funny money. What next? Is our friend Dr Gripp behind this latest episode also?'

'Could be,' said Snaps, 'but let's take it one step at a time.' Then he went to bed. He was tired and weary, but a lot of thoughts went through his mind before he finally got to sleep . . .

Next morning, Snaps woke with a start. A sudden yell from Grandpa jerked his eyes wide open. 'Oh no!' thought Snaps. 'He's not practising his monkey sounds again, is he!' Snaps looked at the clock which Grandpa always kept at Moscow time in case of a nuclear war. Grandpa believed it was very important always to know what time it was in Moscow so as to be able to plan ahead. For example, he said that it was very unlikely that a nuclear war would start before breakfast, because the Russians love large helpings of bacon and eggs. Also, because it takes them so long to warm themselves up in such a cold climate, they would not be in any position even to consider a nuclear strike until after tea-time, and Grandpa was always very nervous at that time of the day which, in England, was at about four o'clock in the morning. However, the most likely time for a nuclear war was, Grandpa believed, at about five past eleven p.m. Moscow time; in other words, just after the vodka shops shut. It was then, Grandpa thought, that the Russians were most irritable, and therefore the more likely to start picking a fight. So Grandpa always scanned the sky for signs of missiles just after the Russian pubs had closed.

Snaps looked again at the clock, which seemed to tick with a Russian accent. A quick calculation told him that it was now seven-thirty, which meant it was lunch-time in Moscow. He heard Grandpa's yell again. Maybe the pubs closed for half-day on Fridays?

Snaps got hastily out of bed and was struggling with his trousers when Grandpa walked in. He was waving an open envelope from which he had just taken a gold-rimmed card.

'Look at this!' he said excitedly. 'It's an invitation to her Majesty's tea-party at Buckingham Palace for my heroic deeds during the war.' Grandpa cleared his throat and, in an important-sounding voice, he read the card aloud: '*To Mr G. Kelly, War Hero. Her Majesty graciously requests the pleasure of your company at her annual tea-party for war veterans at the Palace Gardens on August 11 next. Please arrive early or all the sandwiches will be gone. Dress formal. You may bring a friend if you so desire.* Signed, *H.R.M. Elizabeth.*' Grandpa gave a very satisfied sigh. Snaps gave a sigh of relief also. So it wasn't half-day in Moscow after all.

'Gee, Grandpa,' he said, 'that's great. When did it arrive?'

'Yesterday, I think,' Grandpa answered. 'It must have got pushed under the mat as I was opening the door. Lucky thing I noticed it this morning.' He sniffed the envelope. 'Smells of cat's paws,' he said. Fitzroy gave him a cold stare.

'Watch what you're saying, you old goat,' Fitzroy seemed to say, as he got up smartly and left the room.

'Those cards were all printed at Pilkington's,' Snaps said proudly. 'Which reminds me. I'd better hurry on, if I'm going to be on time.' After a quick helping of *Sugar Snaps* he headed for the lift.

'See you later,' he called to Grandpa as the sliding doors closed. Grandpa was still gazing in ecstasy at his precious gold-rimmed card . . .

The day was beautiful and fresh. The previous night's thunder-storm had really cleared the air. Everything was bright and cheerful under the morning sun.

At Pilkington's, everyone was talking about the phoney banknotes that had been circulated in London. Mr Pilkington told Agnes to be very careful about accepting money in future, especially from strangers, because the police felt that the forger was bound to strike again. Bill Heap asked how, if the forgeries were so good, were they supposed to be able to tell funny banknotes from real ones? Nobody quite knew the answer to that one. So Bill Heap just unwrapped another packet of chewing-gum and went off on his deliveries.

Snaps had lunch with Julie again that day. The grass in the park seemed greener than usual as they strolled along the gravel walk. Snaps explained how he and Grandpa were going to St Davids for the weekend. Julie didn't really like the idea; she thought the whole thing was too risky. She told Snaps to be sure to phone her if anything went wrong.

That afternoon, Mr Pilkington sent Snaps round to the bank to lodge some money before the weekend. He also asked him to bring back some change so as to have some money for customers on Monday morning. When he got to the bank, Snaps found that it had closed for lunch; and it was *still* closed even though it was now well into the afternoon. Outside, a group of people were waiting in bewilderment.

'Is there anyone inside?' someone asked.

Snaps climbed up on to a small ledge and peered through the bank window. Yes, there were people in there all right, and they were in a right state of panic, by the looks of them. Everyone was scurrying to and fro like scalded cats. Mr Moneygall, the Manager, was mopping his brow and talking to his assistant with a worried expression.

'That's odd,' said Snaps. 'I wonder if they've found more forgeries?' He tapped at the window, and Mr Moneygall looked up.

'I want to make a lodgement for Mr Pilkington,' Snaps mimed through the glass, holding up his small bag of banknotes as he did so.

'And get some change as well,' he added.

'Go away from there!' shouted Mr Moneygall. 'We're closed!' And with that, he turned away.

Snaps waited for another half an hour. By then, a large crowd had gathered outside the bank, and they were all in a very irritable humour. Eventually, just before the real closing-time, the doors were opened, and everyone burst inside. Mr Moneygall cheerfully apologized for the delay, and muttered something about a 'slight emergency'. He had a broad smile clipped on to his face, but Snaps could see that he was really a worried man. Every banknote was carefully checked and counted, so Snaps was at the bank for quite a long time. Meanwhile, back at the office, Mr Pilkington was waiting anxiously for him.

'What happened to you, lad?' Mr Pilkington said when Snaps finally arrived. 'I thought you had been kidnapped!'

Snaps handed him the bag of change, and started to tell him about the excitement at the bank.

'More forgeries I bet, as sure as my name is Perkin Pilkington!' exclaimed Mr Pilkington.

'Could be . . .' said Snaps, thoughtfully. But some-how he had the feeling that there was more to this than met the eye . . .

−8−

The Thick Plottens

The sun shone brightly next morning as Snaps and
Grandpa hurried along to Paddington to catch the
early train to Wales. They had decided not to take the
police car because it might attract too much attention.
Also, in view of the very hot weather that was promised,
Grandpa decided not to wear his monkey-suit after all.
Instead, he wore a beautiful tail-coat (complete with
swallow-tails and waistcoat), a pair of trousers with
creases as sharp as a barber's razor, and a beautiful silk
hat. Unfortunately, he couldn't find a suitable shirt
(one that was clean, that is), so he just wore his dickie-
bow on its own. In a small attaché-case he carried the
net and the imitation banana, as well as a flask of tea
and some beetroot sandwiches. These were to be used
during the stake-out that night in St Davids.

They arrived at Paddington station. Grandpa said
that they didn't need to buy tickets because he was
an OAP, so they just jumped the queue and got

straight on to the train. There were a lot of people going away for the weekend, so it was very nice to be able to climb aboard ahead of them all.

Grandpa wondered in which direction the Travellers' Fare Restaurant was. Then, spotting a small red chain above his head, he said: 'Oh well, I think I'll ring for room service.' 'Oh don't, Grandpa!' Snaps shouted. But it was too late. Grandpa had pulled the chain that said: 'Only to be used in emergencies.'

Everybody was thrown around the place as the train driver suddenly slammed on the brakes, thinking that some poor unfortunate infant had fallen overboard. Suitcases came crashing down on to the floor. In the restaurant, the waiter let a sausage fall down the top of a monstrous lady's dress, and as he was wondering how exactly to retrieve it, she slapped him over the head.

When the driver discovered that there was no emergency at all, he was absolutely furious. He asked Grandpa just who did he think he was, going about dressed like Worzel Gummidge, and scaring people to death with his juvenile behaviour. Grandpa said that he didn't mean to scare anybody, that all he wanted was a sandwich and a cup of tea, with two sugars, and maybe a slice of nice cherry cake also, if if wasn't too much trouble. The railway inspector who appeared on the scene told Grandpa to watch his manners or he might have to walk to Wales, and Grandpa had to promise to be on his best behaviour for the remainder of the trip. Eventually, things got back to normal and the train started off again. It went twice as fast as before, trying to make up for lost time.

But Grandpa was still hungry. So he and Snaps went

along to the dining-car. Grandpa had passed the stage where tea, sandwiches and cherry cake could satisfy his appetite. He ordered a monster meal of eggs, sausages, rashers, beans and chips, and endless helpings of brown bread. Snaps was content with a bowl of Rice Krispies and some mashed banana.

'Oh that was gorgeous,' said Grandpa, as he wiped his plate with a chunk of eggy bread, and finished off his tenth cup of tea.

'Grandpa, are you sure we can afford all this? Food is quite expensive on trains, you know.' Snaps's voice had a worried sound to it.

Grandpa winked at him and then he started searching in his waistcoat pocket. Suddenly his face turned rather grave. He rummaged in his tuxedo and then in his razor-sharp trousers.

'Now where the unprintable did I put that mouse!' he muttered.

'Oh no!' gasped Snaps. 'Not again!' He buried his face in his hands. 'Don't you ever carry money with you, Grandpa?' he asked.

'Why sure I do!' said Grandpa, and he took from his pocket the tightly-folded banknote that Dr Gripp had given him. 'I think I'd love something to drink. How about you?'

'Why certainly, but hadn't you better . . .' Grandpa snapped his fingers and the waiter came over.

'A nice cold beer for me,' said Grandpa, 'and some toothrot for the boy.'

'He means some *Coca-Cola*,' Snaps explained.

Presently the waiter brought the drinks. When he had gone, Grandpa slyly reached under the table and untied the lace of his boot. Then he took off his smelly woollen sock (Grandpa *always* wore socks, even in bed) and picked a big piece of toe-nail from the top of his big toe. Snaps sort of guessed what was coming next.

'Watch this,' whispered Grandpa, and he dropped the toe-nail into the frothy beer. When the froth had cleared from the glass, and the dirty piece of toe-nail was clearly visible, Grandpa let out a tremendous screech that brought the waiter scurrying over.

'Is something the matter, sir?' he asked, ever so politely.

'What's this?' asked Grandpa, pointing to the toe-nail.

'Why it looks like a piece of . . .' The waiter wasn't quite sure what it looked like.

'Excuse me, sir,' he said as he hurried away.

Grandpa sat down with a big grin on his face.

'Well, that's that, I suppose,' he said looking rather satisfied with how well things had gone. He lit up a monster cigar, and then reached under the table to put on his boot and sock.

'What appears to be the problem, sir?' a voice said from behind his left shoulder. Grandpa's head spun round. Standing there behind him was the inspector, and he gave Grandpa a look that was as sour as curdled milk. Grandpa pointed to the strange object that was floating in his beer.

'And where do you think that might have come from?' said the inspector, looking under the table at Grandpa's scrawny toes. The inspector's voice was as dry as dish-water. He was determined not to be conned by Grandpa for a second time that day.

'Could I see your ticket, sir?' he asked. Grandpa produced his OAP pass.

'And yours?' he said turning to Snaps.

'He's with me!' said Grandpa, rather sharply.

'I know that,' said the inspector. 'I'm just wondering if he has a ticket. He's hardly an OAP also, now is he? Unless, perhaps, he shrunk a bit recently.' The inspector gave a yellow-toothed grin. Snaps wanted to hit him in the jaw. The inspector turned back to Grandpa and said: 'By the way, sir. I suppose you know that this is a No-Smoking area?'

Just then, the train roared into a tunnel, and the carriage was engulfed in sudden blackness. When it came back into brightness again, Grandpa and Snaps had disappeared.

A swift search failed to find them anywhere. However, one of the toilets was found to be engaged for quite a long time. The inspector, the waiter, and the ticket collector gathered outside.

'It's no use,' called the inspector, 'we know you're in there. Come out with your pants up!' There was no reply from inside the loo.

'OK,' said the inspector, 'if that's the way you want it . . .' Suddenly, the door swung open and the large sausage-lady from the dining-car came out.

'What's the meaning of all this?' she shouted. 'Am I never to have any peace?' And with that, she hammered the inspector with her handbag.

Actually, Snaps and Grandpa were sitting quite comfortably in a first-class carriage, where no one had thought of looking for them. When the train stopped at Swansea, they calmly got off. But just in case of further complications, they quickly got lost in the crowd.

As there was no train service to St Davids, Snaps and Grandpa went by bus. Grandpa, of course, had free travel once more. But Snaps insisted on getting a ticket this time. Tired out by the morning's events, Grandpa fell asleep. Snaps was glad of a break, but he wished Grandpa wouldn't snore so loudly. Soon the bus arrived at St Davids, which turned out to be one of the nicest Welsh cities that Snaps had ever visited. The buildings were old-fashioned and lovely, and as neatly placed as the instruments on a dentist's trolley. It didn't take too long to find Dickson's auctioneering rooms. Almost everyone seemed to be going in that direction, so all Snaps and Grandpa had to do was follow the crowd. As they crossed the square by the old castle, Snaps caught a glimpse of a colourful circus-tent and a battered circus lorry that said *Raymond's Roadshow*. Snaps tugged at Grandpa's sleeve. Grandpa looked and saw the tent being erected for the evening performance. And it was such a convenient site, too, not more than a few hundred yards from the back entrance to Dickson's.

'Aha!' said Grandpa. 'The thick plottens!'

Once inside Dickson's, Snaps and Grandpa casually mingled with the other visitors. The Beatrix Potter books were inside a special glass unit. Snaps studied them carefully. They were beautiful, small, and very portable. Just what the monkey ordered, you might say. And oh so expensive!

'Just imagine,' said Snaps to Grandpa, 'we're looking here at a million quid!'

But Grandpa wasn't listening. He was examining the premises for possible hiding-places. He walked up to a peaked security guard and asked for the loo. He was directed to a small hallway at the back of the shop.

'Come along,' Grandpa called to Snaps. 'I might need your assistance.'

The walls of the hallway were covered in wooden panelling. Grandpa checked out the loo. 'No use hiding there,' he muttered. 'Much too obvious.' There was another door further on. Grandpa opened it. Behind it was a small room which was used for storing mops, buckets and old rags. Only the front portion of the room was visible when the door was opened. The inner section remained in absolute blackness.

'Gammon, aha!' shouted Grandpa. 'Perfect!' Then he closed the door quietly and sauntered away.

Snaps and Grandpa spent the afternoon wandering around St Davids. Time passed rather quickly because there were so many interesting things to see. Just after five o'clock, when the last batch of sightseers were filing into Dickson's, Snaps and Grandpa reckoned it was time to put their plan into action. They queued up once more like casual tourists, and went inside. Actually, their plan went more smoothly than they had expected. They went out to the loo, and then slipped into the small store-room where they crouched down in the darkness. Now, all they had to do was wait.

'Grandpa, Grandpa!' Snaps whispered loudly.

'What is it, my boy? Speak!' answered Grandpa.

'You're standing on my foot!'

'Oh! Sorry 'bout that, chief!'

Soon Dickson's was emptied, and it became so quiet that Grandpa could almost hear his toe-nails grow.

'Oh, well. I reckon it's safe to go out now,' Grandpa said after what seemed like hours. His left knee had gone to sleep, and he began to rub it vigorously.

'You sure?' asked Snaps in a tiny voice.

'Sure I'm sure!' said Grandpa loudly. 'Everyone's been gone for hours!'

Snaps was glad to get out into the half-light of the display room. It was a weird feeling being locked up in total darkness, sort of like being buried alive.

With the swiftness and skill of a conjuror, Grandpa produced a deck of cards and a candle from inside his coat. He lit the candle, placed it carefully on the floor, and then sat down beside it.

'Let's play poker,' he suggested to Snaps. 'It'll pass the time.'

They played for hours. The colour faded from the sky, its blue becoming darker as the world turned herself round a little more. The few high clouds were wispy and ragged, like the wings of storm-battered dragons. Soon, the sideways white eye of the moon looked in through a tiny window above them.

Towards midnight, Snaps and Grandpa had their sandwiches and rather cold tea. They were still sitting on the floor, just out of view of the display unit. Grandpa had placed the imitation banana on top of the square glass box, and the monkey net was positioned on the floor beside him. Grandpa got up to stretch his legs. He took the candle with him on his tour of the room, its small flame cutting a slice in the night. It was a few minutes later, just as Grandpa was sitting down again, that they thought they heard a noise. Grandpa quenched the candle and they crouched down in the darkness. Then they heard it again. It was not really a scratching noise, more of a tapping sound, like the *plic!* of one pool ball snicking another. Then a door opened and an oblong of light fell across the floor. The long beam of a flashlight slowly scanned the room before it came to rest on Grandpa's wrinkled face. A second beam appeared and fell on Snaps.

'I think you'd better come out of there,' a hard voice said. Snaps and Grandpa shaded their eyes and looked up. The loaded revolvers of two security guards were pointing down at them . . .

Grandpa made a run for it! He dashed across the room in a vain effort to escape, but an expert rugby-tackle brought him to the floor. As he fell he hit his head sharply against a solid oak table. Stars appeared. They were closer than he had ever seen them before. He could hear Snaps calling, calling, calling . . . Then he fell through a black hole in space and forgot everything . . .

When he woke up again, he was lying on a small narrow bed in a cell in the St Davids Police Station. It was morning. A bandage was wound round his head. Snaps was sitting beside him. Grandpa sat up with a start.

'Grandpa! You're OK?' asked Snaps excitedly.

'Course I'm OK,' said Grandpa. 'What happened?'

'Don't ask, Grandpa,' Snaps answered. 'We're in a right mess now . . . They think *we* were trying to steal the books in Dickson's . . .'

'What!' roared Grandpa. 'But that's ridiculous!'

'I know,' said Snaps, 'but just look at it from *their* point of view. We're guilty as hell!'

'Tut-tut!' said Grandpa. 'No need to swear! What happens now, I wonder?'

'Don't know. Let's just wait and see . . .'

Later that morning they were taken to another room in the police station for some preliminary questioning. A policeman listened to their story, which lasted for nearly an hour.

'Monkeys?' asked the policeman, when Grandpa had finally finished.

'Yes, monkeys,' repeated Grandpa, in a tone of voice that suggested the whole affair was quite simple really. The policeman leaned back in his chair, dropped his Biro on the report he was writing and slowly let out his breath. Then he leaned forward, knitted his fingers together, and spoke in a kind voice.

'Listen Mr Kelly. I want to help you, I really do. But you've got to give me more than monkeys! OK? Now let's take it from the beginning again . . .' He tore up Grandpa's first statement, and started another.

But Grandpa's story didn't change, and his second account was exactly the same as the first.

'All right,' said the policeman, when Grandpa had finished again. 'That's enough for today . . .'

Just then a second policeman came into the room. By the looks of him he had something important to tell. 'Yes, Constable Stephens. What is it?' asked the policeman at the desk. Constable Stephens held up what looked like a twenty-pound note. 'This was found on one of the suspects. We've just been examining it closely. It's a forgery, sir.'

'What?' shouted Grandpa.

'Oh no!' gasped Snaps.

'Are you sure?' asked the policeman at the desk.

'Almost certain, sir. We haven't got the equipment for a definite examination but if you look closely at it you can see that the paper is of very bad quality. Sort of crumbly, just like the forged notes that were found in London.'

The policeman took the twenty-pound note in his hand and held it up to the light. It was definitely worn, crumbling, disintegrating round the edges. Bits of it fluffed off into his hands, like dry pieces of dust.

'Where did you get this?' he asked sternly.

'Taxi fare,' Grandpa answered.

'You didn't mention that you're a cabby.'

'Well, I'm not exactly a cabby; you see I was working on this special case and I didn't want to take my police car . . .'

'Your police car! So you're a policeman?'

'Well, not exactly either . . . I'm sort of a bit of everything really . . .'

'Including forger, thief and child-corrupter. I bet you have a whole crowd of juveniles working for you in London, just like what's his name . . .?' The policeman's voice was fierce with accusation.

'Hey, hang on a minute,' Snaps interrupted. 'Grandpa's not like that . . .'

'Constable Stephens,' said the desk policeman. 'Get a car ready immediately. This is much too big a case for us to handle. The suspects are going back to London.'

'Yes, sir,' said Constable Stephens. 'Right away, sir . . .'

In all his years living with Grandpa, Snaps had never before had such a crazy, mixed-up weekend. This time, however, he had only himself to blame . . .

−9−

Bank Holiday

There was downright panic in London that Monday when the banks didn't open for business. People of all nationalities gathered on the footpaths hopelessly waiting to get in. There were people with traveller's cheques, stay-at-home cheques, cross cheques, nice cheques, stale cheques and fresh cheques, cheques that would bounce, and cheques that wouldn't. There were people with lots of pounds, and people who were rather thin; people with yens, pens and Biros; people with dollars (most of *them* were scholars); people with marks and sailors with tattoos; people with francs, guilders, lire, pesetas, blue chips, curried chips, strings of pearls, garlic and onions.

Pretty soon, the TV squad arrived, placing microphones under people's noses and asking them how they felt. The managers of the banks remained inside, making rude gestures at the windows. No one had ever seen bank managers acting in this manner before. The situation was obviously rather serious . . .

That day, at about noon, the Governor of the Bank of England, Dr Sterling Gross, went on television to make a special announcement to the nation. London came to a standstill as people rushed to the nearest television set to hear what he had to say. He began by announcing that the lights were going out all over Europe. (It was, in fact, a very sunny day.) Then, with a grave cough and a knitted forehead, he continued:

'As you are no doubt aware, London's banks have been subjected to a flood of phoney banknotes. This is not the first time that the banks have had to deal with a serious problem. In recent years, everyone has been trying to get their hands on our money, but we absolutely refuse to give any of it away. Now we are faced with this new problem, which is, in fact, more serious than anything we've been faced with before.' (He paused for a moment and looked directly into the camera.) 'The banknotes that we thought were forgeries are not actually forgeries at all. They have, in fact, been affected by a strange paper-eating virus which devours the paper and crumbles the banknotes into dust.' There were tears in Dr Sterling's eyes, and a noticeable shake in his voice. His face had the look of the child that Santa Claus forgot. He sniffed and continued. 'But worse still, these microscopic paper-monsters, as I call them, are highly contagious and can multiply rapidly. Our scientists are completely mystified as to where these little monsters have come from. But if they are not stopped, they are liable to devour every scrap of paper in the city. The paper-monsters, I mean, not the scientists. Our experts are currently working on a cure which, they inform me, will be ready some afternoon in the year 2000. In the mean time I ask you all to be as alert and as vigilant as possible. Should you see any signs of crumbly paper, contact your nearest police station, though it will of course be a waste of time. Still, one has to do something. That's the end of this special announcement. Now a look at the weather and the latest score from the Oval where, I believe, England are trailing to Pakistan in the second test . . .'

Dr Sterling's words sent shock waves across the city, not only because England were trailing to Pakistan, but because of the paper-monsters also. Imagine, tiny invisible monsters that actually devoured money! Who could have believed that such a thing was possible? There was consternation in Fleet Street. What if the paper-monsters should strike there!

Sir Zelman Cowen, Chairman of the Press Council, called an emergency meeting for all Fleet Street printers and publishers. Everyone who turned up looked a little under the weather, especially Mr Murdoch, Mr Maxwell and Mr Stevens, who spent most of the meeting bickering at the far end of the conference table. They were the owners of the biggest-selling newspapers in London.

'What shall we do if the paper-monsters get into our newpapers?' they said.

'Into our offices!'

'Our cheque-books!'

'It will be the end of the sports page!'

'The cartoon page!'

'The page-three girl!'

'The end of civilization as we know it!'

Each time they burst into a loud blather, Sir Zelman hammered his gavel and said: 'Gentlemen, please . . . please, gentlemen!' But almost immediately they would start up again with another burst of 'what-ifs' and 'end-ofs', and Sir Zelman would hammer his gavel and say: 'Please, gentlemen . . . gentlemen, please!'

Mr Pilkington, who was standing with Mr Webster at the far end of the crowded room, raised his hand. Sir Zelman pointed to him, and asked for his question.

'What's going to become of us smaller printers, sir?' Mr Pilkington asked. His voice was shaky and nervous. 'I mean, I've been a printer in Fleet Street all my life. So, too, was my father, and his father as well . . . These things, these paper-monsters or whatever they are, could ruin me for ever . . . put an end to the business that took years to build up . . .' Mr Pilkington stopped suddenly. His eyes were glassy and there was a slight tremble in his lower lip. He felt he was going to cry.

'And what about my stamps?' added Mr Webster, who was anxious to highlight the terrible situation he was in. 'What about my prize collections? I've been robbed this summer already. And now this! I could be wiped out overnight. What are we to do, sir? What are we to do?'

Sir Zelman listened to Mr Webster as he gave his short speech and then stumbled into silence. The roomful of people was silent too, waiting for Sir Zelman's reply. He stood up, and spoke firmly, and with authority, like a teacher at school.

'I assure you that everything possible will be done. We will have the full co-operation of the Prime Minister and of the Government. No expense will be spared. Every effort will be made to get to the bottom of this problem, you need have no worries, no worries at all, I assure you.' He tapped the point of his index finger firmly on the table. Then he sat down.

The sudden applause was tremendous. Sir Zelman

raised his hand and stood up again. The room fell silent.

'Anyway, I personally don't really believe that the problem is *that* serious.' he said. There was more monstrous applause as people gave a sigh of relief, reassured by Sir Zelman's encouraging words. Everyone left the room much more hopeful than they were when they entered.

But the problem *was* that serious. Parliament decided that, until the present crisis was over, all printing paper should be confiscated and rationed, just like the tea and sugar during the last war. The result was that paper became scarce and very hard to come by. The newspaper offices were the first to feel the pinch. Because of the scarcity of paper, newspapers got smaller and smaller; they were reduced to one page of tiny print by the end of that week. One by one, the bookshops started to close and to block up their doors in an effort to keep the paper-monsters away. There were stories, rumours and false reports everywhere. When a lady in a bookshop on Charing Cross Road opened a copy of *Easy Cooking*, she found a monster hole in the cheese and onion pizza on page fifty-nine. This story spread like wildfire across the city. Had the paper-monsters gone on the rampage again? Nobody really knew . . . But just in case, Parliament decided that all paper should now only be used in emergencies. Only those people doing important or essential work were allowed to use paper at all. This put the Civil Service out of action immediately. Computer-firms slowed to a halt because they ran out of computer paper. The computer operators sat at their desks, twiddling their thumbs, looking at blank screens. Smokers became very grumpy because of the shortage of cigarette paper, and they tried smoking pipes instead. Toilet-paper was no longer available, and people started sitting further away from each other on buses and trains.

The paper shortage had other effects also. Traffic wardens ran out of tickets, so people started parking anywhere at all, and the traffic problem was a mess. Many chip shops were forced to close because of the shortage of paper bags. No one bought train or bus tickets any more, because there were no more tickets to buy. Everyone hopped aboard without paying anything at all, which was an awful headache for the conductor. Nobody bothered with postage stamps any more and the post office started losing a lot of money. Paper money itself was very, very scarce, and it was very awkward having to carry around a bucketful of coins instead of a walletful of banknotes. People couldn't get married because they couldn't send out invitations and there was no confetti. They couldn't ring each other because there were no directories. Little children sobbed because no one came to their birthday parties, and they got no birthday presents.

And there was still worse to come. It was doubtful whether schools could reopen in the autumn because of the shortage of books, jotters and writing paper. And in the winter, there would probably be an awful lot of chills, colds and flus because there was no tissue paper to catch the germs when people sneezed. And what about Christmas cards, and Santa Claus, and wrapping paper for the presents (if there *were* any presents) and Christmas decorations and crackers and paper hats?

. . . The whole situation was beginning to look very gloomy indeed.

It was approaching the end of August. Snaps and

Grandpa sat idly in their cell in the Tottenham Court Road Police Station. Grandpa had pulled down the lids on his eyes and was taking a quiet snooze. Earlier that day he had received a note from Ms Whetstone (written on an opened-out cigarette packet) which said: 'Glad to hear you've been locked up at last.' Snaps was playing with a pocket computer game. Since his return from St Davids in the police car, he had had numerous visits from Julie who came to see him almost every day. Mr Pilkington and Agnes called on another occasion. So, too, did Mr Henry and Bill Heap. Even Iain dropped in one evening on his way home from work. His hair had grown, and he was puffing a huge pipe. Snaps thought he looked a bit like Huckleberry Finn.

'Gee, you're lucky to be in here (puff) 'cause it's pure chaos outside (puff) ever since this paper-monsters' scare (puff). Who'd 'ave ever thought of such a thing (puff). Imagine monsters that eat paper (puff). We have to put everything away in big plastic bags (cough) and poor Pilkington is a nervous wreck (puff) and Bill Heap is pure hell to work with since the money ran out (cough). How long have you and the old boy here been locked up?'

'Feels like a century . . .' Snaps answered.

'Oh well (puff) think of it as a holiday. We all know you're innocent (puff). Well, cheerio. No, it's OK. I'll let myself out (splutter).'

The officer in charge of the police station happened to be Detective Sergeant Tom Tibbles, an old friend of Grandpa's who was shortly to retire. They often played chess together till late into the night, and each day Tom Tibbles kept Snaps and Grandpa informed as to how their case was progressing.

'You know we had nothing to do with this paper-monsters thing, don't you, Tom? Sure, I may cheat at chess now and again, and stuff like that . . . But defraud the entire city? Not blooming likely!' Snaps, Grandpa and Tom Tibbles were having breakfast together. Tom Tibbles put down the spoon which he was just about to dig into his soft-boiled egg.

'I know, I know,' he said. 'But all the same, you were both found in Dickson's rooms, and they're pretty sore because you managed to break through their security so simply. Also, you have a pile of other offences . . .' (He gave Grandpa a very dirty look.) 'Resisting arrest, defrauding British Rail of two breakfasts, stealing a taxi, driving a police car without a licence, picking your toes in public places . . . The list goes on and on.' Tom Tibbles looked straight into Grandpa's beady eyes. 'Listen. I've done all I can to help you. When you were brought here, I told them to go easy on you. When they searched your house, I told them not to make too much of a mess. I even told them to feed your cat, for goodness' sake! I told them to leave you your police car, but they took it away. There's really nothing else I can do . . .'

'But they found nothing in my house?'

'No, not as far as I know.'

'Well, that proves we're innocent, doesn't it?'

'Maybe, but it's not up to me to decide. Listen, I've only until Christmas left at this job. Don't expect me to do anything that will make them take away my pension. OK?'

'OK, OK. But just one small favour. OK?'

'Depends what it is.'

Grandpa quickly removed his boot, and took a rolled-up piece of card from inside his sock.

'I've been hiding this between my toes,' he said with

a chuckle. 'Not even those paper-monsters would dare go in there!' He handed the piece of card to Tom Tibbles. It was the invitation Grandpa had received to Her Majesty's garden party. It was folded up tight as a corpse's eye. 'Can we go, Tom?' Grandpa said. 'Me and the boy here? Just one day out on bail, with as many policemen as you like. Just one day. What do you say?'

Tom Tibbles took the invitation and looked at it closely.

'Hmmmm. It *is* from Her Majesty. I'll see what I can do. I'll take it to my superiors just to see what they say, but I'm not making any promises, mind you!'

Two days later, when Tom Tibbles brought in breakfast, he was grinning like a Cheshire cat. Grandpa and Snaps were to be allowed to attend the garden party after all! But, of course, they had to make a solemn promise to behave themselves, and not to try to escape. Just to make sure that they didn't, two plain-clothes detectives would accompany them. Grandpa had also to promise not to drink all the wine, to pick fights or his nose, or to remove his boots in public.

On the morning of their departure, a special message arrived from Buckingham Palace. It said that, because of the paper shortage, there might not be enough napkins, decorations, or paper cups, but that there would be plenty of food, drinks and balloons. People were advised to bring along their own cups, if at all possible. (They could quite easily do *without* napkins or decorations.) Also, *please! please!* dress respectably. Neither Snaps nor Grandpa worried too much about the decorations or paper cups. They were delighted to be free, if only for a day. They looked a right pair of swells in their suits, shirts, ties and shiny footwear as they were driven off in the big black shiny limousine heading for Buckingham Palace . . .

— IO —

Dicing with Death

But, of course, Grandpa had no intention of going back to prison. As he and Snaps headed towards Buckingham Palace, his bright eyes were twinkling, and his busy brain was searching for a plan . . . He whispered to Snaps to be ready to run for it as soon as he gave the word. Poor Snaps was astounded.

'But you promised Tom Tibbles you'd come back,' he whispered, hoping that the two police detectives in the front of the car hadn't heard him.

'And so I will. So I will,' said Grandpa. 'Only not today . . .'

'Well, you could at least have left him a note . . .'

'How could I? No paper! Anyway, don't worry about it. We'll explain everything just as soon as we've got to the bottom of this.'

Snaps and Grandpa were accompanied by two detectives called Detective Fox, and Detective Duckworth. They were both middle-aged and very cagey. It would be difficult enough to shake them off. Still, nothing was impossible for Grandpa Kelly!

Firstly, while going in the gates of the Palace, he whispered to one of the security guards that there were two strange men trying to gatecrash the party. But once Detectives Fox and Duckworth had shown their badges, they were allowed inside immediately. 'Oh well,' sighed Grandpa, 'it was worth a try . . .'

The Palace gardens were a frenzy of colour. The beautiful flowers were in bloom, and Grandpa immediately picked one of the white carnations and put it in his buttonhole. There were people everywhere. Old ladies greeted each other, hugged, and rubbed their ears together. Old men wandered around like lost penguins. There were lashings of food, drink, peanuts and crisps. Soon, Her Majesty appeared and shook hands with all of the guests. Snaps was worried that Grandpa might do something embarrassing. But he didn't, and Snaps was very relieved.

Actually, Grandpa was too busy with thinking about a plan of escape. He tried just about everything. He hid in the shrubbery, in the flower-bed, under the long table, in the gents' toilet, in the ladies' toilet, behind the garden statues, behind the garden seats, but each time they found him. He even tried climbing a tree, but all to no avail. He would hide inside the Palace if only he could get in, but there were too many attendants knocking around. And besides, Detectives Fox and Duckworth never took their eyes off him . . .

Then he found it; the magic word, the golden ticket, the Open Sesame! There was an ambulance parked over at the far end of the railings. It had been brought along in case any of the old people should get sick.

Grandpa grinned at Snaps, and then squinted up at the blazing sun.

'Perfect day for a heat-stroke, don't you think?' he said. Then, after letting out a tremendous roar of agony he fell to the ground. For a few seconds, he kicked, wriggled, and said unprintable words. Then he lay suddenly still. He was rushed to the ambulance where he was wired up to all sorts of strange-looking contraptions. The young doctor and nurse were determined to save his life. Snaps and Detective Fox climbed into the ambulance and sat close to the dying man. Detective Duckworth followed behind in the limousine. Then, with its siren blazing, the ambulance rushed out of the Palace gates towards the nearest hospital.

Everyone was slightly surprised when the dying man suddenly sat up and, with eyes as mad as hatter's, stared at Detective Fox. Snaps had the strange feeling that Detective Fox was about to be sent on a wild goose chase. 'The doors . . .' gasped Grandpa. 'They're not properly closed . . . (gasp) . . .' Detective Fox leaned over. He opened the ambulance doors and was just about to bang them soundly when *thump*! Grandpa's boot caught him right on the bum. Detective Fox went into orbit. Grandpa looked at the young nurse.

'It's OK,' he said. 'There'll be a bus along in a minute . . . Now, if you'll excuse me . . .' He unhooked himself from all the contraptions, and as soon as the ambulance slowed down to a reasonable speed, Snaps and Grandpa leaped off and went running away through the streets.

For the rest of that day they kept out of sight in alleys, doorways and deserted warehouses. The day gave up its hold reluctantly, but slowly, very slowly, night-time came. Snaps wondered whether it was really a good idea to have run away like that. Now they *really* looked guilty. Their pictures would be flashed into a million homes and policemen would be on the lookout everywhere. Meanwhile, the real criminals, Dr Gripp and his monkeys, were left completely free.

When twilight fell, Snaps and Grandpa huddled together outside the window of a video shop waiting for the evening news. Straight away, their faces appeared on the TV screen that flickered out on to the street.

'Gee, they didn't waste any time, did they?' Snaps said.

'No. Come on, let's get out of here,' Grandpa answered.

'Hang on a minute,' Snaps said tugging Grandpa by the sleeve. 'There's something else.'

It was a news item about another outburst of paper-monsters in a shop on Tottenham Court Road. Snaps knew this shop quite well. He often used to go there on his day-off to browse around looking at the unusual rows of funny-looking objects. Everything in the shop was made from paper. There were aeroplanes, puppets, animals, ships, dolls, trains, cars, garages, rows and rows of soldiers, skyscrapers, castles and windmills. There were masks, fake heads, and sore thumbs that you put on over your own thumb. In fact there was just about every toy you could mention, and all of them were cleverly made from paper. The TV camera focused on the desolate shelves. Many of the paper toys still looked OK, but they crumbled into dust as soon as the TV reporter touched them. The owner of the shop was pale and almost speechless. He held up a toy soldier whose left leg was completely eaten away. 'We must do something to stop this terrible disease,' he sobbed. 'We must do something before it's too late.'

'Surely they don't think *we're* responsible for all that?' Snaps said, pointing to the collection of ruined toys on the TV screen.

'Course they do!' said Grandpa. 'But we're the only ones that can do anything about the whole thing before it *really* gets out of hand.'

'Seems to me that it's out of hand already,' Snaps mumbled as they turned down a side-street.

'First thing we've got to do is get a set of wheels. We can't travel by train, bus or taxi. And they've taken away our car. So we've got to go back and get my motorbike.'

'Your motorbike!' said Snaps. 'You don't mean that heap of junk you keep beside your bed?'

'What do you mean that "heap of junk"? Have you seen it recently?'

'Well, no. It's always covered with a sheet . . .'

'Then there's a surprise in store for you, my lad. Just let's hope that they haven't taken it away!'

They went back to Fitzroy Square taking the loneliest route possible. They scurried down side-streets, through derelict buildings, and climbed over walls. Soon, they arrived back at their house. It was still being guarded by the police. A young policeman stood at the front door, chatting across to another policeman who was on a motorbike. The rear entrance to the house was being watched by two policemen in a car.

'What now?' asked Snaps, as he peeped around the corner of a building at the edge of the Square. Grandpa surveyed the situation. Then he looked up at the night sky. Suddenly he saw it, the yellow arm of a crane reaching across the street at the side of their house, and his eyes began to shine like two mad moons.

'C'mon!' he whispered loudly. 'We're going home!'

An extension was being built on to the bank at Grafton Street, directly opposite the side of Snaps's and Grandpa's house. If they could manage to turn the crane ever so slightly, then its huge arm would reach right across Grafton Street and make a bridge directly on to their roof. And who'd suspect that they could come through that way!

Snaps and Grandpa scurried away under cover of darkness. They stole into the yard at the back of the bank and climbed up into the crane. With a bit of luck the keys might still be in it . . . They were! Grandpa looked at Snaps and gave an enthusiastic grin. So far so good. Now how do these things work?

The engine of the crane was surprisingly quiet for something that was so big. The noise it made was also easily deadened by the sound of the traffic below. 'Here goes,' said Grandpa, and he expertly swung the great arm across the street. If anyone had looked up at that moment, they might have wondered why a crane was still working at this time of night. But no one seemed to notice, least of all the policemen who were on careful watch below.

'Now comes the hard part,' Grandpa said, and for the first time that day his voice sounded a little worried. 'You want to go first, or will I?' Snaps gave Grandpa the look that he usually reserved for new varieties of spiders.

'Honestly, Grandpa. You give me the cold horrors sometimes,' he said.

Snaps peered over the edge of the crane-driver's cab. They were about five storeys up, not really a great distance, but high enough all the same should you happen to fall. Thud! Down you would go like a sack of apples addressed *Special Delivery* to gravity. And, as everyone knows, too much gravity is bad for the health. (Poor Humpty Dumpty died from an overdose of it.) Still, there could be no going back now that they had gone this far. It was all or nothing from here on.

'OK,' Snaps sighed. 'I'll go first.'

'That's the spirit, my boy! There's nothing to it really. Just don't look down. And try not to think of Humpty Dumpty. Anyway, I'm sure that story has been exaggerated.'

Snaps climbed up, and then inched his way along the arm of the crane. Above him the moon was a clipped toe-nail, and the growing night was soft, silver, serene. Somewhere in the distance, an aeroplane whistled, to conceal its fear of gravity. Snaps's senses were like sharpened pencils, but deep in his rib-cage a mechanical monkey was playing strange notes on his heart-strings. Snaps kept crawling, while beneath him the tangle of traffic hummed its mantra like medieval monks. Inch by inch he went, slowly, nervously along the cold steel arm of the crane. Then he saw it, a few inches away from him, and about half as big as his hand. It was a spider. His blood froze, and a curtain flapped in his brain. He closed his eyes suddenly and then jerked them open again. The spider was still there, its long legs making their awful spindly move-ment. Come off it, Snaps. It can't be real. You don't get spiders that big in London. Certainly not up here. Oh boy, why did it have to be spiders!

Snaps was suddenly awake again. The fright had done him good. He considered how best to deal with the situation. 'If I don't do something quickly, I could be up here all night. Reach out maybe, and with a sudden jerk of the hand, flick it over. But what if it doesn't fall? What if it just stays there?'

Then his eye caught another movement, a sudden flicker of white on the distant end of the crane arm. Something else was coming towards him, slowly, menacingly, green eyes piercing the night like splintered steel. It was Fitzroy! Snaps nearly lost his grip, he felt so excited at seeing his old friend. With the skill and daring of an acrobat, Fitzroy pounced on the huge spider, shook it fiercely in his needle teeth, and then let it fall lifeless through the night. Then all his attention turned towards Snaps. He miaowwwed loudly, walked on a bit, then turned round as if imploring Snaps to follow. Snaps had spent about enough time on that metal bridge, and he really wanted to get off. Then taking a monster breath he crawled quickly, firmly and successfully over to the other side. He had made it! He was home! In the east, high over the city, a shooting star blazed brightly, like the sweep of an artist's paint-brush, across the darkened sky.

Snaps turned around to encourage Grandpa. But Grandpa was already half-way across, not crawling but running, with the slick steps of a dancer, his eyes filled with zany fire. With a sudden leap through the air, Grandpa landed on the roof, and he did a nice little somersault to finish. All three congratulated one another for their daring success. Then, quietly opening the trapdoor, they climbed down inside.

It was the policeman at the front door of the house

who first thought he heard something. He turned into the hallway and listened again. There was the soft thud of a door being closed, and the quiet whirring sound of a motor. The policeman looked up towards the small changing numbers. There was someone coming down in the lift. The policeman waited. Four ... three ... two ... one ... ground floor. There was a moment of silence in which nothing happened. Then **BLAST-OFF!** The door of the lift slid open and a monster motorbike came thundering into the hallway.

'Holy smoke!' shouted the policeman. He had just about time to jump out of the way of this roaring monster which descended the steps in a flash and then zoomed into the street with the speed of a sideways rocket.

'Calling all units! Calling all units!' the policeman shouted into his mouthpiece. 'Possible suspects heading north along Tottenham Court Road. Request back-up immediately!'

Every police car cruising in the area turned and converged upon the West End of London. Soon, there were police cars everywhere, lights shining, sirens vicious, like evil hungry sharks. But Grandpa's motor-bike was no easy prey. He zoomed down the steps of the underground pedestrian crossing and zipped along in the direction of the tube station. The huge engine echoed through the confined space of the underground alley, like an angry lion marauding through a dungeon. People were scattered in all directions, and the 'blind' musician at the corner had just about time to gather up his hatful of pennies when he saw Grandpa coming.

Down and down they went, faster and faster, passing the amazed ticket collector on their way to the underground train. 'Hey! Where's your fare?' the collector called out as Grandpa flashed past. 'Don't need one!' Grandpa shouted. 'I'm an old-age pensioner. I can travel free!'

There was a train just about to pull off from the platform. Grandpa revved up his motorbike and they just made it through the automatic doors.

'Phew! That was close!' gasped Snaps as he climbed off the pillion seat. A dozen heads turned and looked at them in amazement.

'What's all the long faces for?' Grandpa shouted, and the heads immediately turned away again.

Snaps and Grandpa travelled safely out of the city centre. They came up again somewhere near Fulham. The night was now quiet and sleepy. There were very few people around. They had decided that it would be safer to split up for a few days. Snaps rang Julie from the first phonebox they could find that wasn't vandalized. She offered to put him up for a few nights until the heat went out of the situation.

Grandpa dropped Snaps off under the light at the street corner where Julie lived. It was just a short walk to her house.

'Where are you going to go, Grandpa?' Snaps asked.

'A place I know,' Grandpa answered with a wink.

'But how will I find you?'

'You won't!' answered Grandpa, rearranging his goggles. 'I'll find *you*!' And, with that, he zoomed off into the night . . .

— I I —

Uninvited Guest

As soon as Julie's mother had gone out, Snaps came
out from his hiding-place in the garage. He had made
himself comfortable there curled up on an old discarded
armchair, and he had slept quite well. At some time
during the night he had been awakened by the wail of
a police siren, and he thought they were coming for
him. But the sound soon trailed off into the distance
and Snaps went back to sleep.

Next morning, Julie rang the library to say that she
wouldn't be coming to work, so she and Snaps could
spend the day together. They spent the morning sitting
around chatting, listening to records and playing
dominoes. After lunch Snaps began to feel a little
jittery. He wanted to go into town. 'But that would be
too dangerous,' Julie protested. 'What if they catch
you?'

'I'll go in disguise,' Snaps answered.

'Then I'm coming with you,' Julie said enthusiastically. 'The police are looking for an old man and a boy, not a boy and girl. No one will ever suspect us! And let's get some camouflage for a start. You look much too respectable!'

They decided to disguise themselves completely. Julie cut chunks off Snaps's hair, which had grown quite long throughout the summer. Then she spiked it and coloured it with green dye. She gave him a T-shirt, jacket and raggy jeans, and a chain and yellow socks to finish off the outfit. He was almost unrecognizable. Then she set about transforming herself with bright-pink lipstick, too much eye-shadow, lots of powder, some ear-rings, a fantastic shirt, a bright skirt and shocking shoes.

'How do I look?' she asked when she had finished.

'Absolutely terrible,' said Snaps, and they both laughed. 'Well, here goes,' he added, as he opened the door.

Nobody gave them the slightest bit of attention, not on the bus or in the underground, or anywhere. They looked just like a couple of ordinary colourful young-sters. At Piccadilly Circus a policeman called after them: 'Excuse me, miss . . .' and Snaps's heart almost stopped with fright. Then the policeman handed Julie the fingerless glove she had dropped on the ground. Julie thanked him, and they continued on their way.

They could get no chips later because the chip shops were closed. Snaps decided he'd like to go and see Mr Pilkington, so they headed off in that direction.

As they came near Fleet Street, a stream of police cars went whizzing by with lights flashing and sirens blaring. 'Wonder what's up?' Snaps said to Julie, and they asked a person who was coming from the Fleet Street direction. 'An emergency in Fleet Street,' the stranger said. 'In Pilkington's, I think. It's those blessed paper-monsters again. It's absolutely terrible that . . .'

Snaps and Julie didn't wait for the stranger to finish. They went running down the street towards Pilkington's. When they got there, a crowd of people had already gathered outside, and the police were trying to keep everybody back. A group of men in white space-suits, gloves and helmets, were carrying bundles of books from Mr Pilkington's shop and were loading them into vans that had wire grilles on the windows. The loading went on until the complete shop had been emptied, and the entire shelves were bare. Then the vans departed again, escorted by the police. Gradually the crowd of people thinned out, and continued on their way.

Snaps waited until the last policeman had left. Then he ran across the road and into the shop. Mr Pilkington was sitting alone among the deserted shelves. The printing-machine was silent, and it looked like the other workers had already left.

'I'm afraid we're closed for business,' Mr Pilkington said, looking up.

'It's me, Mr Pilkington,' Snaps said. 'Don't you recognize me?'

Mr Pilkington refocused.

'Why, it's Snaps. But why are you in fancy-dress?'

'It's a long story, sir. I'd like you to meet my friend Julie.'

'How do you do? But I'm afraid I'm in no mood for a social call, as you can see.'

Snaps looked around. The big lower room of the printing-works, with its smells of ink and years-old papery debris, looked desolate and untidy. It also felt very odd without the prattle of people and the clattering noise.

'What's happened?' Snaps asked. Mr Pilkington sighed.

'They came this afternoon to do a routine check on our stock of books. I was here on my own because we haven't been operating normally since the paper shortage. Anyway, one of the inspectors noticed some frayed edges on one of my antique books, and when he opened it he found it was falling to pieces . . . So he notified the Paper Emergency Squad, who came and took the lot away.'

'What are they going to do with them, the books I mean?' Snaps asked. 'They're not going to burn them, I hope.'

Mr Pilkington looked astounded. 'Oh, good heavens no!' he said. 'They're going to do some tests to see the extent of the damage. But if it's those paper-monsters, I'm afraid there's very little hope. The books will all be destroyed anyway.'

Mr Pilkington placed his hands over his face. 'And I took such care,' he continued. 'I thought I might be one of the lucky ones. But now my life is ruined . . . ruined.'

Snaps placed his hand on Mr Pilkington's shoulder. 'Don't worry,' he said. 'I'm sure everything will be all right.' But he didn't even believe it himself.

Snaps felt very sorry for Mr Pilkington as he left his shop.

We've got to do something to stop this outrage,' he said to Julie as they sipped a Coke in McDonald's.

'What *can* we do?' Julie asked.

'I'm going down to Dr Gripp's house tonight. I'm sure he's behind all this mess.'

'OK. But I'm coming with you.'

'No. You've got to stay behind, just in case I get caught. If I get safely in and out, then I'll ring you immediately. If I don't, then you ring the police and tell them the full story. OK?'

Julie wasn't happy about this plan, but she agreed all the same. She insisted on going with him that night as far as Greenwich, just in case something should happen on the way. The bus dropped them not far from Dr Gripp's mansion. They said goodbye, and Julie crossed the road to get the bus back to London.

It was another dry, sweltering night. There were lots of boats sleeping in the harbour, and the moon was a ghostly galleon anchored in the sky. Snaps wasn't quite sure what his plan of action would be. He only knew that he had to get inside Dr Gripp's house and look for definite clues that would tie in with the recent robberies, and with the paper-monsters as well. He sighed. It wasn't going to be an easy task. Still, he would have to try.

Getting in was the first problem. Dr Gripp's house was a real fortress, like something out of the Middle Ages. High walls surrounded it on all sides, and on one side there was also the river. He stepped down to the water's edge. An ugly gargoyle looked down at him from the top corner of the wall. Snaps held on, then leaned out as far as he could without falling into the water. 'Hey, there's a door there, further down towards the wharves,' he muttered to himself. It was one of those big old-fashioned ones, like you see on castles. He strained himself to get a better look. 'No use. Need a boat.' He looked up and down the river. A small rubber-dinghy nestled between two trim cruisers. Slowly, silently, he untied it, and then lay waiting. No sound, so no one had heard. He let the river carry him to the base of Dr Gripp's wall, using the small oars only to keep himself on course. He made his way past two other cruisers and finally stopped in front of the old door, just out of sight of the wharves. The big padlock on the door looked impressive, but nobody seemed to realize that the small look-out hole was unbarred, and big enough for him to get in by. He searched the dinghy's cubby-hole for a rope and an anchor. He found both. Pretty small, but perfect all the same. He swung, threw and missed. The anchor fell with a splash. He tried again. It caught. He climbed up with some difficulty, the old hinges grating. He could not believe it was all so easy after all.

Once inside the garden, Snaps hid for a moment behind an exotic-looking tree, not making a sound. Then he drove himself onwards at a lurching run, over the flowers, over the daisy-studded lawn. The grass had not been cut and it snatched at his feet.

He was in view of the front door. Another short run would bring him to the house itself. He headed around the back. It was darker there, more shadowy. There was a shed with its door slightly open. Perhaps it led directly into the house? He went in. There was another slight creak of hinges but his own nerves had turned to tempered steel. A flight of stairs led up to the house and he could see a small light shining through the door at the top of it. Slowly he climbed, step by step, his cropped hair bristling like some sort of night-creature.

He reached the top, halted, listened. No sound except his own pulse beating. He pushed the door slightly. It led on to a sumptuous hallway. He was inside Dr Gripp's house! He had to go the whole way now. He had to search everywhere, every inch, until he found the room full of the stolen treasures.

After an age of scurrying down dusty corridors, through darkened rooms and doorways he found it – the treasure room!

It was dark, mysterious, and very cool. He turned on the light, expecting nothing. But the room came alive like a cinema screen. The walls were lined with animal heads: rhinos, tigers and lions. Old photographs and trophies lined the marble fireplace, and a beautiful animal rug decorated the floor.

A large oval table stood like an island in the centre of the room; around it were anchored eight tall chairs, like ships in a harbour.

There were huge portraits of people from another age, heavy tables, chairs and a gorgeous sofa. And there by the window, as brazen as you like, laid out as if for display, were the rows of stolen treasures: Mr Webster's stamps, the Devon papyrus, the library books, the Cambridge scrolls, Shakespeare's poem, the paper hat, the lot! 'So I was right!' Snaps said to himself. 'What time is it?' He spun round and looked at the old clock above the mantelpiece. Two o'clock, the time of night when dreams become reality! 'Must contact the police,' he said. 'Get them here before . . .' Then he noticed the whirr of the air-conditioning. 'No wonder it's so cool in here,' he thought, as he turned to leave. But someone colder than air-conditioning was standing at the door . . .

'Snaps Kelly, I believe?' a voice said. It was Dr Gripp!

'The game's over, Gripp. You might as well hand yourself over to the police.' Snaps tried to sound as cool as a TV detective; but he knew that, really, he only sounded stupid. Dr Gripp completely ignored his words.

'You've been admiring my treasures, I see,' he said in a dry voice.

'*Your* treasures!' exclaimed Snaps. 'The country's treasures, you mean!'

'And there are more to come,' continued Dr Gripp.

'Yeah, like Beatrix Potter's books . . .' Snaps didn't like being ignored.

'No, I don't think so,' said Dr Gripp. 'You see, I've the good sense to check whether or not there are security guards before I burgle a place. Which is more than I can say about *you*.' He gave Snaps the sort of look that he had not seen since he left school. Snaps wanted to lash out, and beat, and bite . . .

'Still, it was quite intelligent of you to figure out how we were doing it, myself and Raymond, I mean. And of course, the monkeys. Not even the police have figured it out yet . . .' He gave a little laugh. Then he continued talking, as if to himself. 'Well, what choice had I, really?' he asked with a pained expression. 'Did you expect me to leave all those treasures lying around to be destroyed when I knew what was going to happen? I'm a humane man, Mr Kelly; I couldn't stand by and watch those terrible paper-monsters devour *everything*!'

'Don't you Mr Kelly me!' Snaps's voice was sharp as a razor. 'You've stolen from Mr Webster, a good friend of mine. And Mr Pilkington's shop was emptied out today, the only man in London who would give me a job! And the whole city's in a state of panic, all because of you and your paper-monsters . . .' Snaps was red with rage.

'*My* paper-monster's,' said Dr Gripp coolly. 'What makes you think that they're *my* paper-monsters?'

'Oh, come off it!' shouted Snaps. 'I may be Irish, but I'm not an idiot. I don't know how you've done it. I just know you *have*. And I don't know why. I'll tell you something, Dr Whateveryoucallyourself, I've watched you on telly, on the scientific programme. But you're no scientist. You're nothing but a fraud, just like that funny money you've been passing around. Only a stupid fraud . . .'

Dr Gripp's voice became suddenly as cold as a snowman's heart attack, and his face was a stark and frozen landscape.

'A fraud!' he hissed. 'You call me a fraud. I, one of the world's best scientists, who has made a discovery that nobody yet knows about, a discovery that could save this world from destruction, and you call me a fraud!' He rushed over to the huge window. Outside, in the distance, the lights of London were twinkling. Dr Gripp pointed.

'Out there are twelve million people. Each person makes a ton of rubbish every year, most of it paper. That's twelve million tons of paper rubbish each year. Consider, for a moment, the humble paper bag. The trees from which it is made took a hundred years to form and cannot be replaced. The bag will be in use for perhaps an hour or two, maybe less. Then it will be thrown away. Then it becomes rubbish, a nuisance, something we despise. And we have to spend millions of pounds each year getting rid of our rubbish. The whole thing is ridiculous. We spend a hundred years growing a tree – most of us weren't even born when these trees were started – and all for what? To make rubbish, that's what.

'Or consider, even, the ordinary milk-carton. It too is made from mashed-up wood-pulp, from trees that took perhaps a hundred years to grow. Just think of those ancient roots reaching deep down into the heart of the earth. Yet the milk-carton will be in use for no more than a few short hours. That will be the end of it. If it ends up on a rubbish tip it will swell the world's growing garbage mountain. Years from now it will still be there. If, in an attempt to beat the garbage problem, it is burned at the tip-head, it will give off dangerous fumes which are among the most feared in the world. We are slowly destroying ourselves in a sea of garbage, and you call *me* a fraud.'

Snaps thought for a moment, and then said:

'Well, I can see your point, but all the same . . .'

Dr Gripp spun round.

'There are no buts!' he shouted fiercely. 'All I want to do is rid the world of its filth, destroy the rubbish, clean the slate, and start all over again. Then we can do it right next time.'

'Yes, but you're destroying more than paper-bags and milk-cartons. Can't you see? The whole city is in a state of terror. People have been put out of work, libraries have been closed down, there are not enough schoolbooks for the children . . . Do you really have to do it this way?'

'Of course! There is always a price to pay. What I'm offering will be painful at the start. But everyone will thank me in the end, when the world is clean again!

Anyway, all of our libraries are full of junk. Am I expected to spare all the rubbish for the sake of a masterpiece or two? I've done all I can. I can do no more . . .'

'But you're destroying all the money. People work, but they get no pay . . .'

'Money! One of humanity's worst inventions! People steal from each other, cheat each other, even kill each other, for money! Life will be much better when I've got rid of it all!'

'But money feeds the world! It buys clothes, books, food for children . . .'

'Yes! And it also pays for weapons of war and destruction!'

There was no use in arguing with him. Snaps could see that. 'This guy's a bit crazy,' Snaps thought to himself. 'I'd better try to humour him . . .

'Where do they come from anyway, these paper-monsters, or whatever they are? How come no one can see them, not even the scientists with microscopes and things?' Snaps was genuinely interested. In his mind he was making a note of everything Dr Gripp was saying. It would all have to be repeated in court later. Still, he couldn't help feeling sorry for him.

'No one can see them because they're invisible,' Dr Gripp answered with a grin.

'Invisible? How do you mean, invisible? Nothing is invisible, really . . .'

'Oh, no?' Dr Gripp moved to the window again, and pointed at the sky. 'Look at all those stars, those tiny specks in the sky. All we have to do is look up, and there they are, we can see them. Yet, for every star we can see, there is another that we can't see at all. Not because it's not there, mind you, but because it's too remote, minute and tiny. No telescope on earth can show it up. Yet it's there in all its glory, a splendid, invisible creation.' Dr Gripp turned and looked at Snaps. His voice became more threatening. 'It's the same thing with my paper-monsters. They're tiny creatures. There is no microscope powerful enough to show us what they look like. Yet, they exist. Tiny, invisible, but deadly. And it was I who discovered them!'

'This guy is really weird,' thought Snaps. 'There's no point in talking to him any more. I might as well start trying to get out of here . . .'

'Well, thank you for the free lecture,' he said with a sort of half smile. 'I think it's time I was getting along. It's quite late. I won't keep you up any longer . . .'

Dr Gripp laughed, and for an instant his face looked almost human. 'Well you've got a sense of humour anyway. I like a person with a sense of humour. But do you really think I'm going to let you go now, after all I've just told you? You could have a tape-recorder in your pocket. Perhaps you've recorded everything I've just said?'

'Tape-recorder? What tape-recorder? I've got no tape-recorder. . . Look!' Snaps showed him his empty pockets.

'I see! So you haven't! Still, it wouldn't have made much difference. You're not leaving here.'

'Oh, yeah? Then who's going to stop me?'

'My men.'

'Your men? What men? I don't see any men. Where are they? Are they invisible too?'

Dr Gripp laughed.

'No, they're not invisible. You'll see them soon

enough.' He walked to the heavy desk and pressed a button. He smiled at Snaps, a dark, sinister smile. Snaps thought it was about time he was leaving. He ran to the door. But it was too late! Two hefty bouncers were there to grab him. Snaps wriggled, tugged and struggled. But it was no use. They had him firmly caught in their monstrous hands.

'Take him to the zoo,' Dr Gripp said sharply. And Snaps was quickly frog-marched away . . .

— 12 —

Under a Blood-red Sky

'Grandpa!'

'Snaps!'

'Grandpa!'

'Snaps!'

'Grandpa!'

'OK,' said Grandpa. 'Let's not overdo it, the welcome bit, I mean . . . But what are *you* doing here?'

'But I was about to ask you the same question.'

'Were you really? Well, go ahead and ask it then.'

'What are *you* doing here?'

'I came here to investigate this Gripp chap. But I got myself bonked over the head.' He touched a visible lump on the back of his baldy patch. 'OOOh, that's sore,' he said with a grimace. 'I told him that my pal Snaps would come to rescue me. But now you've got yourself arrested too . . .'

'So *that's* how he knew my name. I was wondering about that bit . . . Now how do we get out of here?'

'We don't. I've been trying since yesterday. It's useless . . .' Grandpa thought for a moment. 'At least I think it was yesterday?' he said with a puzzled expression. 'It's hard to tell what time it is in here. It *is* tomorrow now, isn't it? I mean, it's not still yesterday?'

'Of course it's not still yesterday,' said Snaps. 'It's today.'

'Well, that means it *is* tomorrow,' said Grandpa excitedly. 'Because if *I* thought today was still yesterday, when in fact it's today, then that means that it's really tomorrow. So I was right after all!'

'Relax, Grandpa. Relax. I think it's *now* we should be worrying about.'

Snaps paced around the deserted room.

'I wonder why he said we were going to the zoo?'

'Oh, goody!' said Grandpa, and he started to sing: 'We'll all going to the zoo tomorrow, zoo tomorrow, zoo tomorrow . . . Or is it today? Or maybe we went there yesterday? I just can't seem to remember !'

There was a strange noise on the far side of the wall, a sort of scratching sound and the vibration of voices. Snaps also thought he heard a snarl. Neither Snaps nor Grandpa had realized that there was a small sliding door in the far corner of the room. It was so well-camouflaged they hadn't noticed it. The door slid open, and a square black hole appeared where the wall used to be.

'Must be feeding time,' said Snaps.

'But I hope, *we're* not on the menu,' added Grandpa doubtfully.

A small, shadowy figure appeared at the square entrance.

'Come in, if you're good-looking,' said Grandpa. The head and shoulders of a monkey protruded into the room. It eyed Grandpa closely, gibbered a little, and then gave a vicious snarl.

'Nasty-looking devil, isn't he?' said Grandpa.

'Looks hungry, too,' added Snaps with a gulp.

'Still, it's nice of him to come and keep us company.'

'Hang on a minute, I think he's brought along a few of his friends.' There was the chatter of animal voices from the small entrance, and one by one, eight other monkeys came into the room. They paced up and down, slowly, menacingly, their eyes fixed firmly on Grandpa and Snaps. Occasionally, their chatter changed to a high-pitched shriek, and the horrible lips were pulled back to reveal huge yellow teeth.

Suddenly, a huge bolt was slid across, and the door quickly opened. Snaps and Grandpa fell backwards into a dimly-lit hallway and the door was suddenly slammed again. The terrible scratching of claws and nails re-echoed through the house. Snaps and Grandpa got up. A tiny man, no bigger than a child, stood beside them.

'Who the unprintable are you?' asked Grandpa in an amazed voice.

'I'm Raymond,' answered the man. 'But hurry! There's no time to talk now. Quickly, follow me!' Snaps thought he detected an American accent.

They were led down the hallway and out into the sort of shed that Snaps had been in already that night. Then Raymond pointed to the door that led on to the river.

'It's open now,' he said. 'You can escape through there. I've left a boat waiting. Go quickly. And good luck!' He turned to go away.

'Hang on a minute,' shouted Grandpa, grabbing

him by the arm. 'You've got some explaining to do. Like why did you let us out? And who's Gripp anyway? And what in the name of Mike is going on around here?'

'OK, OK, stop squeezing my arm. That hurts, you know. Ow!'

Grandpa released his grip a little, but his eyes still looked fierce and serious. Raymond the midget decided he'd better do some talking.

'Now what I want you to understand is that I had nothing to do with all this paper-monster stuff. That was all *his* idea, you know. Absolutely nothing to do with me. He came to me some time ago and asked would I like to make a little extra cash by simply transporting some specially trained monkeys. I already had a few monkeys in my circus, so I said what the heck. A few more can only improve things. My circus had got sort of run-down, you know, and I really needed the bit of extra cash. Then we started into petty crime. Nothing too big at first, you understand. Just the odd small robbery or two, just to keep life interesting. At the start I didn't like it, the robbing, I mean. But then I said: "Raymond, old chap, no one's ever done you any favours, so where's the harm in stealing a little bit from people who have too much already!" At the start, everything worked like a dream. I mean the monkeys did everything. Don't ask me where he got them, 'cause I don't know. He never told me much about that side of things . . .'

Raymond stopped talking for a moment. Then he listened for any strange sounds. When he was happy that no one was listening apart from Snaps and Grandpa, he continued.

'It was earlier this summer that things started to go wrong. He began planning bigger and bigger jobs, ones that were a lot riskier. Like the museum. And Webster's. And other places as well, you probably know them all by now. Not only that, but he started hoarding the stuff. Usually we'd sell our loot to an American guy I knew. But we stopped doing that. He wouldn't let me, and the jobs just got crazier and crazier. I mean, I don't mind a bit of small honest crime. But he just got out of hand altogether. Really, he did . . .'

'What do you know about the paper-monsters?' asked Grandpa.

'Absolutely nothing. That, too, was entirely his idea. I don't know how he does it. Or why. I know that the monkeys are involved in some way. But don't ask me how . . . He's hired a crowd of heavy guys to guard him, and to look after the running of this place. I don't know how he can afford to pay them, 'cause he's sold none of his stolen stuff at all recently. It's all hoarded inside the house. He's gone absolutely crazy, and I want nothing further to do with him. I can't leave him just yet, not until I'm sure it's absolutely safe . . .'

'How are you going to explain our escape?' asked Snaps.

'Don't worry. I'll think of something,' answered Raymond with a half smile.

'Does he have any other accomplices, apart from his henchmen, I mean?' asked Grandpa.

'Not that I know of,' said Raymond. 'He's a real loner, a recluse. However, I once remember seeing a name written into his diary when I was tidying his desk one day. A Professor Chaudhuri, of Delhi University in India. I think this chap was once a colleague of Dr

Gripp's. I know he must be someone important because Dr Gripp snapped the diary from me as soon as he entered the room. And he was very suspicious of me for days afterwards. I've a funny feeling that this Professor Chaudhuri might be able to provide a vital clue to the paper-monsters' scare.'

'Would you be prepared to tell the police all of this?' Grandpa asked.

'Of course I would!' said Raymond emphatically. 'I'm absolutely sick of the whole thing. Only we've got to do it right. We've got to find evidence that he's responsible for the paper-monsters. Also, and just as important, we've got to find a cure.'

'You're right,' said Snaps. 'We'll have to move fast, before it's too late. Grandad, we've got to go to India and find this Chaudhuri chap. He's our only hope!'

'Hey, wait a minute. What do you mean, go to India? It's not just down the road, you know. You've got to *fly* there. In an aeroplane. And I've never been up in one of those things in my life!'

'Well, just think of it as a new adventure,' said Snaps.

'No, you can include me out, I'm afraid,' Grandpa answered.

'But Grandpa . . .'

'OK. I'll give you a definite *maybe*, but that's my final offer.'

'Then I'll go alone, or perhaps Julie will come with me. We've got to find Professor Chaudhuri. We've just *got* to!'

'Hold on, hold on,' Raymond interrupted. 'Do you really understand what you're taking on here? India is a vast country. It has millions and millions of people.

It's not going to be that easy to find one man. And suppose you *don't* find him? What if he's dead, or has left the country, or has simply disappeared? What then? You'll have made all that journey simply for nothing.'

'But he can't be dead. He just can't be. If he were, well why would Dr Gripp have been so afraid of you discovering the name in his diary?'

'OK, well suppose he's not dead. And suppose by some miracle you do succeed in finding him. What if he *can't* help us? What if he knows nothing about these paper-monsters or how to stop them?'

'Well, he knows Dr Gripp, doesn't he? Really, he might be our only chance . . .'

Snaps looked imploringly at Grandpa and then at Raymond. They could see that there was no use in arguing with him any more. Raymond sighed.

'Perhaps you're right. It's a brave thing you're doing, win or lose.'

'Listen!' Grandpa interrupted.

There was the sound of footsteps, and the rumble of heavy doors.

'Get going!' said Raymond. 'Run as fast as you can. Good luck!'

'Thanks,' said Snaps earnestly. 'We won't forget your help.'

Snaps and Grandpa scampered across the silent lawn.

The boat was waiting, just as Raymond had said. When Snaps was safely aboard, Grandpa fiddled with the motor. The water churned up behind them as the motor burst into life. Grandpa turned the boat in a wide arc and headed speedily for the city which was still listlessly dreaming under the blood-red sky. The traffic hummed along the Old Brompton Road. But Snaps and Grandpa were tired, so they let the river do the singing . . .

—13—

A Passage to India

Next morning when Snaps arrived at Heathrow Airport, Grandpa was already there waiting for him. He was wearing a smile that you could post a letter in. Beside him was a large suitcase.

'What are *you* so happy about?' Snaps asked.

'Why, because we're going away, of course,' said Grandpa. 'Travel broadens the mind, as the old philosophers used to say. It is the only true educator. It breaks down social barriers and opens new windows on to life. It . . .'

'Hang on a minute,' Snaps interrupted. 'Let's get a few things sorted out before you take off on a flight of poetic fantasy. What's in the suitcase?'

'The world is all that is in the case,' Grandpa said proudly as he undid the zipper and revealed a large deflated globe. 'Just in case we get lost, you know . . .'

Snaps sniffed the air. Grandpa smelt like the leftovers from a walrus's picnic.

'Grandpa,' said Snaps, 'what is that awful smell? Have you been having sardines for breakfast again? And why have you your shirt on back to front?'

'Smell? What smell?' Grandpa's wily nostrils gave a few hearty sniffs. 'Oh, *that* smell. It's not from me, it's from *him*.' Grandpa pulled back the ragged flap of his jacket, and revealed Fitzroy bundled up inside his waistcoat. 'I think he spent the night exploring some very interesting dustbins,' Grandpa added with a grin. Snaps sighed.

'Grandpa, what is Fitzroy doing here? You *know* we can't take him with us.'

'Course we can. Cats have a great sense of direction. If anyone can find Professor Cloud-hurry . . .'

'Chaudhuri.'

'Yes, that's what I said. Fitzroy will take us straight to him. Besides, this cat is part Siamese, you know. He can visit all his old ancestors in India. It will be just like going home, a special treat for a poor old feline who's never been a mile from London. Remember Dick Whittington's cat, called what's-his-name? He brought his master good luck wherever he went.'

'But he never travelled to India by plane,' said Snaps. 'Listen Grandpa, be reasonable. I think we should be as discreet as possible. You know, the police are still probably looking for us. It's my guess that they're here in this very airport at this very moment watching out for a young boy and his grandfather.'

'Ha–ha,' Grandpa said in a voice as sharp as a surgeon's saw, 'but they're *not* looking out for a Christian minister who is heading back to his mission in India.' Grandpa pointed to his priest's collar. 'I'm the Very Reverend G. Kennedy (notice the clever change of name). I'm very pleased to meet you, young man. Will you be my assistant on the Lord's important work?'

'Oh no,' Snaps thought. 'Here we go again.' That was the trouble with Grandpa. You could sometimes turn him off, but you could never plug him out.

'*Flight 105 to New Delhi Now Boarding at Gate Thirteen,*' the announcer said.

'Come on, my boy. Time to rush.' Grandpa settled his secret bundle under his jacket and headed off for Gate Thirteen. Snaps, as nervous as a mousetrap, scampered after him.

But actually, things went much better than Snaps had expected. They got through the first check-point without any difficulty, but with Grandpa showering blessings in all directions.

However, walking through the metal-detector, that's where their problems began. Snaps went first carrying Grandpa's suitcase.

Then came Grandpa with his two tins of *Meow Mix* (cats love it), and with his electric tooth-brush concealed in his pocket. The metal-detector suddenly sprang into life, like the guards at Buckingham Palace when the Princess of Wales happens to walk by.

'Would you step this way, Yur Reverence.' The supervisor's voice was straight from the freezer: cold and hard. He was joined by uniformed assistants with faces that looked as cheerless as a wet blanket. The forbidden objects were removed from Grandpa's pockets; and, of course, when he raised his arms to be frisked, Fitzroy burst free. (The cat was out of the bag, you might say . . .)

'Holy mackerel,' gasped one of the assistants.

132

'Grab that cat,' shouted another.

But Fitzroy, whose great-grandfather had once worked for Harry Houdini, was already planning his escape. He darted about the room, doing loop-de-loops over the luggage like a real circus cat. Then, unfortunately, he jumped on to the conveyor-belt, and started some on-the-spot jogging. Grandpa went over and lifted him up. Fitzroy would have to remain behind. Grandpa thought for a moment, and then insisted on one condition, which the supervisor agreed to. With that, Snaps and Grandpa headed for their plane, and Fitzroy was taken back to London by taxi, a means of transport Dick Whittington's cat *never* experienced; no, not even on the day he went to London to see the Queen . . .

When the air hostess came with breakfast, Grandpa chose a big German sausage and as there were no *Sugar Snaps* on board, Snaps had two bowls of *Bermuda Triangles* instead.

'Don't you think it's a bit risky having those *Bermuda Triangles* during a plane flight?' Grandpa asked as he bit into his tranquil sausage.

'Course not,' said Snaps. 'I'm hungry. Anyway, we're going in the opposite direction. And besides, with *you* on board, *nothing* would dare mess with us.'

'No, I suppose not,' said Grandpa, and he gave the sort of grin that would make an accordion jealous.

After breakfast, Snaps felt a lot happier. But he was still very tired. He leaned back into the soft reclining seat, closed his eyes, and fell into a deep sleep.

Snaps suddenly woke up, and raised himself on his elbow.

'Look.' Grandpa pointed out of the window of the plane. Far below them was the blue sea, and the heart-shaped landscape of India.

'We're here,' said Grandpa. 'And to prove it: we've arrived.'

Soon, they were inside the huge, busy Arrivals Area; they collected their luggage and headed outside.

'Now, I wonder if there are any taxis? We've got to find Professor Cloud-hurry.'

'Cloud-hurry?' said Snaps, in a questioning voice.

'Hurry?' repeated Grandpa. 'Yes, I suppose we'd better. We haven't much time.' And with that, he scampered across the tarmac towards the line of waiting taxis.

There were plenty of taxis in Delhi, but some of them were very rattly. The car that Grandpa and Snaps got into was like a blob of heated colour on the thickly-crowded streets. Occasionally, it lurched forward with a sudden burst of speed, but more usually, it inched its way through the city like a lobster with a limp. At ten miles an hour it whined like a spinning-top, and rattled Grandpa's kidneys like dice in a box.

'Holy cow,' said Grandpa. 'It's hot in here.' He mopped his wrinkled temples with one of the gaudy handkerchiefs he had bartered from a trader. Then, to pass the time, he burst into verses of poetry: 'Oh, to be in England when the winds of March doth blow ... Oh how I love poetry! You can beat an egg, but you can't beat a good poem, or a good breeze, pheeww!'

The sun stared down like an angry eye. They were glad when, some hours later, they finally ground to a halt outside the building where Professor Chaudhuri lived.

But he was no longer there. Nor was he at any of the

other destinations that Snaps and Grandpa were directed to. For three days they searched but to no avail. At night they slept in cheap lodging-houses, where Snaps lay awake for hours listening to Grandpa's empty stomach rattle its chains.

'Never mind, my boy,' Grandpa would say cheerfully as he lay curled up on the hard floor. 'Some people feel like this *all* the time.'

On the fourth day they learned that Professor Chaudhuri had moved to a place called Kalimpong somewhere in the Himalayas. (This was told to them by a rather grumpy landlady.)

So later that day, a young boy and his grandfather could be seen hitching a lift out of Delhi. They were picked up by a jolly tanker-driver who brought them all the way across the country.

They were now right in the middle of the Himalayas.

They could see Everest, as well as the other runners-up in the world's tallest mountain competition. But more important still, they could see Kalimpong, nestling among mountains that tower and loom. The road they were on led straight down into it.

'Let's go, my boy,' said Grandpa. 'We're almost there.'

A short distance down the road, Grandpa spotted a rough eating-house called *The Great Blondino's*. He suggested to Snaps that they rest for a while, and get something to eat. They could still reach Kalimpong before nightfall.

Inside, the place was deserted, except for a surprised-looking Blondino, and a small boy, probably his son. Blondino was delighted to have such unexpected guests. He gave Snaps and Grandpa a *great* welcome, and cooked them a *great* meal. (Truly, this *was* the Great Blondino.)

'I don't suppose this chap knows Professor Chaudhuri?' Grandpa said later.

'Bit too much of a long shot. Still, there's no harm in asking.'

'Chaudhuri?' repeated Blondino, when Snaps had explained the reason for the trip across half a continent.

'There are many Chaudhuris in this country.'

'Like Kellys in Ireland,' added Grandpa.

'Yes, but this chap's a bit special,' Snaps continued. 'He's a retired professor from Delhi or somewhere. We're not too sure exactly. We must find him. He's living somewhere in these parts, or so we have been told.'

'Ah, *Professor* Chaudhuri,' said Blondino, his face lighting up like a Christmas tree, 'the one who lives in the mountains. Surely this must be the man you are looking for?'

Grandpa nearly choked on his piece of whatever-it-was.

'You don't mean to say . . .'

'. . . that I know him? Yes, I know him. He moved to these parts about a year ago. He lives the life of a hermit in the mountains.'

Blondino gestured vaguely with his hand. Then he called the small boy over and said something to him in his own language. The boy immediately scampered out of the door.

'See, I told you,' Grandpa said to Snaps. 'I told you we'd find him.'

'Where does he live? I mean where can we find

him?' Snaps asked Blondino eagerly. He could hardly believe they had finally got so close.

'I don't know exactly,' Blondino answered, 'but I think the boy can help. The professor has a helper, a small orphan who minds the goats for him. My son saw this boy just this very day, not more than three hours ago. I've sent him to try to find him again. Then he will take you to this man you seek so much. In the mean time, come and sit on the porch. The view of the town and of the mountains is magnificent at this time of evening.'

They sat for what seemed like hours, but still Blondino's son did not return. Snaps was no longer conscious of the view of the mountains. His only thought was to find Chaudhuri. They couldn't fail now that they had got so close.

The light had disappeared from the sky. The sun was a boiled potato which made one final lunge before dropping back into the saucepan of mountains. The strange whirring of busy night-creatures was beginning to haunt the world. Suddenly, Snaps sat up.

'I think I see something,' he said.

Grandpa peered into the half-gloom with eyes as intense as bare electric wires. Yes, there *was* someone making his way up the incline. Snaps looked again. There were two figures, actually. One was Blondino's son; the other was a stranger. They emerged into the lantern hiss of the porch. They were both tattered and dusty; it had obviously been a long trip.

Blondino's son said something to his father, who then turned to Snaps and Grandpa.

'This is Chaudhuri's helper. My son has found him for you.' (Blondino spoke seriously and with pride.)

'This child cannot speak, but he will take you to see his master. Your search, at last, is over.'

There was a hint of sadness in Blondino's voice as he said goodbye to his two new friends. He would accept no payment for his hospitality; it was his pleasure and duty to be of service. After a warm-hearted farewell, Snaps and Grandpa followed their young guide out into the night.

The small boy may have been unable to speak, but there was nothing the matter with his eyes. He led Snaps and Grandpa through the darkness with the skill of a night-creature. Up and up they travelled, until they were deep in the mountains. For a while, the lights of Kalimpong twinkled in the distance, but were soon only a stain in the distant sky. Presently the moon came out to light their way. It was a cold moon, whose light made night-owls shiver and change their minds. Once, they passed a magnificent brown deer that was drinking at a water-hole, so close they could have reached out and touched his slurp. Snaps shuddered as he wondered whether there were still tigers in India. Every time a twig snapped, his hair climbed a tree.

Up and up they went, into the Himalayan night, the dark at the top of the stairs. The thin crisp air vibrated like a hive and white stars pimpled the universe. It was easy to imagine that the stars were bees. It was easy to imagine that the moon was a queen bee, and that the night stored up its secrets like honey.

Then they saw it, the small hut with its lit window. The small boy stood and pointed. Even in the pimply light of the moon they could see how snug a little haven it was, with its bean-poles, its beehives, its fenced-off area of fertile garden.

They headed down the small incline as fast as their legs could manage. Even Grandpa turned on a sudden burst of speed, and took off like a jack-rabbit. The orphan boy pushed open the door, and Snaps walked slowly into the dimly lit room. This was it, the moment of truth. Grandpa entered too, and stood behind Snaps in the shadows. On a mat, under a small lantern, sat an elegant gentleman, dressed in an immaculate white shirt.

'Professor Chaudhuri, I presume?' Snaps said, when his voice came back to him. The man looked up at Snaps and Grandpa, two strange creatures from the outside world. Then he nodded, and stood up, arms outstretched, to welcome them . . .

— 14 —

The Full Story

'So you want to know about Samuel Gripp? I will tell
you. He was one of my most distinguished colleagues.
He was not always a bad man. You must understand
that.' Professor Chaudhuri was sitting cross-legged at a
low table. Snaps and Grandpa were sitting opposite
him, listening intently. The orphan boy was somewhere
in the background. It was the next morning, and they
were all eating breakfast. Snaps had slept soundly the
night before. Not even the strange sounds of mountain
creatures were enough to disturb him. Grandpa too
looked bright as a button. Professor Chaudhuri picked
a fingerful of maize from his small bowl, and then
continued talking.

'I first met him after he had won an important
scholarship to the Gandhi Scientific Centre in Delhi.
He came there to do research. Science, for him, was
not really work; it was his love, his joy and recreation.
In fact, it was his entire life. Later he specialized in

zoology, which was my particular subject also. (I was Professor of Zoology at the Gandhi Centre.) It was then that he started his research into Primates: apes, monkeys and gorillas. He was particularly interested in the lesser Mongolian monkeys, which are reckoned to be among the most intelligent animals in the world. They are also quite vicious . . .'

'Yes, I know,' said Snaps.

'For two years Sam and myself travelled all over Asia, wherever the lesser Mongolians were to be found. We studied them closely, recording their habits and peculiarities. Once, I got very sick from a fever, and Sam spent many days minding and caring for me. Eventually, when he thought I might die, he carried me through miles of dense jungle to a nearby medical centre. From there I was whisked away to the nearest hospital. I now realize that I owe him my life. Without his assistance, I would not be alive today.'

'Gosh!' said Snaps. 'He can't be *all* bad, in that case!'

'He was *never* a bad man,' Professor Chaudhuri insisted. 'He was dedicated always to the welfare of mankind. Anyway, soon after we left the jungle Sam published a book about the Mongolian monkeys, which became quite well-known among university men.'

'Yes, we've heard of that book,' said Snaps. 'Something about parasites, wasn't it?'

'That's correct,' said the professor. 'Parasites. Those creatures that live off other creatures. Things like fleas, bugs and insects. Which brings me to the second part of my story . . .

'After his book was published, Sam became recognized as quite a specialist on monkeys. Then an event happened which was to mark a turning-point in his life. It was at the start of the Russian space programme, when monkeys were being sent into space. Sam was approached by a group of Russian scientists who were studying the effects of space travel on animal life. They asked him to become head of their team, and they offered him a vast sum of money. Sam was, of course, the obvious person for the job. He accepted the offer, not because of the money, you know, but because of the opportunity to further his research. He appointed me as his chief assistant. Funny, isn't it, how things turn around? Anyway, for some time after that we did research on monkeys that had travelled through space.

'It was near the end of our stay in Russia that Sam realized something that he had never really thought of until then. His special interest had always been parasites, yet he had completely overlooked the fact that when monkeys travel through space they don't travel alone. They bring with them all the bugs, fleas and other parasites that they've picked up in the jungle. These all get a free ride in the rocket! Now, wouldn't it be interesting, thought Sam, to study the effects of space travel on them also. So that's exactly what he started to do.

'At first, nothing very exciting was shown up in our microscopes. I don't know exactly what we expected to find, maybe some tiny green-headed monsters or something like that. Yet we never found anything irregular. All the fleas, bugs and insects that we examined were exactly the same after their trip through space as they were before they left the earth. In the end, it all became a bit boring.

'Then, one day at the end of a hard session in the

laboratory, a strange thing happened. It was late at night, and we were both very tired. I had spent most of the day in the catalogue room, while Sam was at the microscope. The other members of our team had all left. I remember coming from the catalogue room and seeing Sam with the little glass slide held delicately between his fingers. On it were some particles of dust which he had taken from one of the space monkeys. As he was about to place it in the microscope the glass slipped from his fingers and tinkled on to the floor. "Don't you think it's time you called it a day?" I said to him. "Yes, you're right," he said with a sigh. Then he scraped up the particles of dust off the floor, folded them into a piece of paper and left them on his desk.

'The next morning, a most peculiar thing had happened. As he unfolded the piece of paper, it crumbled in his fingers. It had been completely destroyed in the night. Sam was puzzled. He showed me the pieces of dusty fragments, and together we tried to find what had caused the paper to disintegrate so quickly. The dust itself contained no obvious clues. So that night we decided to do a little experiment. Fragments of dust were taken from the space monkeys again and left in an envelope overnight. The next day, when we went to the laboratory, we found that the same thing had happened: the envelope had been completely eaten away.

'I needn't tell you that we were totally stunned. We combed carefully through the monkeys' fur and examined hundreds of bugs, fleas and other parasites – some of which were smaller than the head of a pin – but we found none that could devour paper so quickly. Then we thought that perhaps the monkeys had brought back some strange minute monsters from outer space, but we could find no evidence for this. Then it suddenly dawned on us. The answer was not here in the laboratory at all, but outside in the forest.'

The professor stopped talking for a moment, and pointed through the window towards the dense, distant trees.

'The monkeys we used for our space experiments came from some of the deepest forests in Asia. On their backs, hiding snugly in their fur, they carried all the usual bugs and parasites, but some unusual ones as well. Some of these tiny creatures had been carried through space on the backs of the monkeys, just like the other parasites we examined, only these particular ones had somehow been transformed by their trip. Their ability to devour organic material had been mysteriously speeded up. They could now complete a year's work in one single night. We didn't know exactly how this had been made possible. We could only guess that their transformation had something to do with the fantastic speed of the rocket as it hurtled through space. In astronomy, such things are not completely unheard of. We know, for example, that speed affects age and the passage of time. An astronaut who has travelled through space is a few seconds younger than he would have been had he never left the earth. As far as we knew, this was exactly what had happened to the spaced-out parasites, or the paper-monsters, as you call them. Their devouring action had been speeded up by their space-odyssey, and they could now breed and multiply much more rapidly.

'Of course, once Sam and I discovered this, we became very worried. It was much too dangerous to experiment any further, especially as we knew so little. Whole forests might have been wiped out if these creatures had escaped. So we placed all of the space-monkeys in strict quarantine and I think we succeeded in killing off all of the dangerous bacteria that we had discovered. Still, just to be on the safe side, the surviving monkeys were not released back into the jungle. It would have been much too risky. Instead, they were kept in captivity for the rest of their lives . . . Of course, all of this was kept strictly secret. No one knew about the paper-eating bacteria, except, of course myself and Sam, and one or two higher officials in the Kremlin.

'That was about the last time I saw Sam. He remained in Russia for a time, and later we lost touch altogether. I went back to my job in Delhi. For a while, I was Professor of Pulp and Paper Technology at a university in Australia. But, I was getting old. I was becoming tired of everything, even science. I was completely disgusted at the uses to which science was being put, I mean the manufacture of nuclear arms and other weapons of destruction. I needed to get away, to start a new life, before it was too late. So I came here. I built myself this simple home, started my garden and my beehives, and lived alone far away from the cares of the world. Then one day the boy came. He is an orphan. His parents were both drowned in a boating accident at sea, and he has never spoken since that day. He lives with me. He minds my goats, and helps me tend to my garden. He never speaks, but he listens to me and to my stories. I have given him a slate and a rough piece of chalk so that he can communicate with me. But, so far, he has written nothing. His story was told to me by a man in Kalimpong. I sometimes have to go there for supplies. Still, I think that he is happy, in spite of all. His name is Dhani. That means wealth.'

Professor Chaudhuri stopped talking, and they sat in silence for a moment or two. Through the window there came the screech of some exotic bird. Then Snaps said:

'Dr Samuel Gripp obviously didn't destroy *all* the bacteria that you discovered. He must have kept some hidden away that you didn't know about?'

'Obviously,' said the professor. 'But I'm sure he had his reasons . . .'

'But he must have a cure for them,' said Grandpa. 'Otherwise how can he stop the paper-monsters from completely getting out of hand?'

'Big bugs have little bugs on their backs to bite them,' said the professor. 'Little bugs have lesser bugs, and so on *ad infinitum.*'

'I beg your pardon?' said Snaps.

'What I mean is,' explained the professor, 'everything is preyed on by something else. That is the law of nature, and of the natural world. Even parasites have their parasites, you know!'

'You mean, these monsters that devour paper also have other monsters that devour them?'

'Quite obviously! Look here . . .'

Professor Chaudhuri went towards a small desk which held an array of scientific instruments. He selected a specimen-glass from his huge collection, and placed it in his microscope.

'This glass contains a paper-scorpion,' he said, as he turned the small wheel and focused.

'A *what?*' Snaps and Grandpa both asked together.

'A paper-scorpion,' the professor repeated.

'What's a paper-scorpion?' asked Snaps.

The professor looked up, took off his glasses and said:

'Well, a paper-scorpion is any of a large group of tiny arachnids usually found among fallen leaves or under the bark of dead trees. This particular species . . .' (he gestured towards the microscope) '. . . is called *Chelifer cancroides*, and is often found in homes and libraries where it preys on insects that eat books. Other species live in caves or birds' nests, and a few inhabit ant nests.'

'Wow,' said Snaps. 'I never knew such creatures existed.'

'Nasty-looking little critter,' said Grandpa, as he peered down into the microscope.

The professor continued: 'Paper-scorpions resemble true scorpions, except that they have no tail or sting. They feed on insects, spiders and bookworms that are killed by an injection of poison from the paper-scorpion's pincers. The paper-scorpion eats almost everything that is smaller than itself, but its favourite dish is the bookworm. The bookworm is the common name for the larvae of certain insects injurious to books. Great damage is done by the insect order *Corrodentia*, the book-lice. Two species in particular – *Troctes divinatorius* and *Atropos pulsatoria* are especially fond of the glue used in bookbinding . . .'

'You mean they sniff it?' Grandpa interrupted.

'No,' said the professor. 'They eat it. Paper-scorpions mate in springtime when . . .'

'OK, OK,' said Grandpa. 'No need for the sex talk. There are young children present, you know.'

'Gosh,' said Snaps. 'So you reckon it's some of those book-lice larvae that Dr Gripp has released in London?'

'Almost certainly,' Professor Chaudhuri said with authority. 'Book-lice are creatures of the forest floor, but they have migrated to every library in the world, or to any other place where books are stored. Even your ordinary daily newspaper contains millions of them.'

'But how is it that the bacteria released in London are *invisible*?' Snaps asked.

'Most bacteria *are* invisible,' explained the professor. 'Even among the order of book-lice, for every specimen that we *can* see, there are dozens more that we *can't*.'

'Gosh!' said Snaps, pretending that he understood, even though he really didn't. 'I wonder why Gripp waited until now to release them, the paper-monsters I mean.'

'I have a feeling that the answer to that has something to do with the heat-wave we've been having in England this summer,' said Grandpa. 'These creatures come from the jungle, you know, so they probably need heat to survive.'

'Yes, you're probably correct,' said the professor. 'But that still doesn't answer the question as to why he released them in the first place?'

'Oh, some sort of strange notion about cleaning up the world,' said Snaps remembering his first – and last – conversation with Dr Gripp. 'But the important question *now* is what are *we* going to do to stop him, before he goes too far?' Snaps turned to the professor.

'You've got to come back to England with us,' he said. 'You must speak to him. You're probably the only person in the whole world whom he will listen to!'

'No, no. I cannot,' said the professor. 'My place is here. You can have my story, or any other help I can give, but don't ask me to go back with you. I was never a great traveller. Besides, I've given up all that sort of thing. I just want to live here in peace, just me and the boy.'

'But you've already said that you travelled to many places,' said Snaps.

'Yes, but I'm not a traveller at heart. I'm just a casual gypsy wandering out from my base and back. In the old days I travelled for the sake of science. But that's all over. I'm too old now. Who would mind my garden and my goats? And what about my house? No, I must stay here . . . This is where I belong.'

'But you *must* come!' Snaps implored, 'If not for our sake, then at least for the sake of science . . .'

But Professor Chaudhuri gestured that he was no longer listening.

Throughout all this conversation, the boy Dhani had sat silently in the background, and they were almost unaware of his existence. It was only when he made a noise reaching for the slate and rough piece of chalk that they remembered he was still there. He gathered himself into the corner and curled himself round the slate as he wrote. He made his letters slowly and with care. When he was finished, he held the slate out to the professor. Then he sat back with his head lying against one angled shoulder, staring at the man. His eyes were hard and bright, of a glittering sea-colour. Professor Chaudhuri read the carefully written note:

'You must go. You must. I will mind the goats. And the garden. And the house.'

The professor laughed, his dark eyes full of sympathy. 'Great souls suffer in silence, and great minds think alike,' he said to Dhani. 'But they don't know what they're taking on, Dhani my child . . .'

Like a puppet lifted on its strings, the small boy rose from his seat in the corner. He took the slate again and wrote: 'Then you must help them.' His eyes stared fixedly at the professor's face. The professor laughed and said:

'You're a strange child, Dhani. An unknown quantity in so many ways. I wonder what you would have turned out like had you not been made to suffer so much ... Or what my life would have been like if you hadn't arrived.'

The professor's eyes were filled with a strange new light. He continued: 'But, as this is your first time to speak to me, in words rather than in signs, and as this is your first request, I will not turn it down. I will go with these people because *you* ask me to. Who knows, perhaps it will all work out for the best.'

That afternoon was spent in a golden haze, shot through with talk and laughter. As evening came, Professor Chaudhuri gathered together the few things he would need for the journey. He took some clothes, some books, and a small leather bag full of forest leaves. Then, waving goodbye to the small silent figure in the doorway, Snaps, Grandpa and Professor Chaudhuri headed down the mountain . . .

— 15 —

High Jinx

It was now September, and already the leaves were
changing colour after the hot, searing summer. The
schools had not yet reopened because of the paper
shortage. There was not a schoolbook to be had in
London. Thousands of books had been devoured by the
paper-monsters, and those that had survived were locked
away in safes, attics and basements until this strange
epidemic was over. There were no longer any comics,
newspapers or magazines as all of London's newsagents
had been closed for many weeks. Children were becoming
very stupid from watching too much TV, and very bored
also. It looked like there would be no books, puzzles or
jigsaws for Christmas, and no rockets or bangers at Guy
Fawkes. The situation was very serious indeed.

It was early in the afternoon as Snaps and Julie
walked across the park. The afternoon sky looked like a
brain: moist, grey, confused wisps of cloud straying
across it like thoughts. A mad-scientist sun probed at

the brain, making it bob and quiver as if immersed in a tank of strange liquids. The park was a forlorn landscape, empty of laughter and children, filled with decaying leaves. Ahead of them, a small boy was struggling with the wreck of a paper kite. The kite was in a bad state of decay. What was left of it was raggy and torn and was held together with sticky tape. The small boy ran along into the breeze, but the kite refused to fly. It just bumped clumsily along the ground. The small boy left it there, and went sadly home.

Snaps and Julie were headed for Grandpa's new home. Grandpa was now living in the trailer of an articulated lorry. Snaps didn't know where he got it, and he didn't bother to ask. Grandpa now called himself Elvis Kelly, the Hottest Trucker in the West End, and he spoke in a funny language on his CB radio to other truckers who passed along the way. His favourite person was a coloured driver called Big Eddie, who drove a huge diesel lorry which said *Highly Inflammable* on the side. Every day, Grandpa and Big Eddie would talk to each other on their radios. And every night, Grandpa parked his lorry and trailer (the trailer was nicknamed *High Jinx*) in a different layby or parking-lot, so as not to attract the attention of the police.

At the moment, *High Jinx* was stationed at the southern edge of Hyde Park. Snaps and Julie were heading back there after a morning in town. There wasn't much to do in town any more, as most of the shops were closed. London was slowly becoming a ghost town; all that was missing was the tumble-weed. Still, there was no litter on the streets; no nice posters reminding us about films, shows and concerts. The paper-monsters had devoured them all.

High Jinx was parked among a row of other trailers and articulated trucks, so it was very nicely camouflaged. Inside, it was beautiful, bright and comfortable. It was also very spacious. There was plenty of room for everybody: for Snaps, Grandpa and Professor Chaudhuri. And for Julie also, who came to visit almost every day. At the moment, the trailer looked like a laboratory on wheels, it was so filled with scientific equipment. Since the professor arrived, they had been trying to find ways of halting the march of the paper-monsters; but so far, every experiment had failed.

Then, of course, there was the usual problem of Grandpa. Grandpa was a creature of chaos, always the star of his own mad movie, always headed on that train that only stops on the far side of the moon. It amazed Snaps how Grandpa and the professor had ever managed to work together at all. The professor's mind was slow and logical. Each step he took was carefully calculated, like a thief with delicate fingers slowly cracking a safe. But Grandpa's mind rushed forward like a mad white river, and strange thoughts, like iguanas, basked upon the shore. Nevertheless, they had both worked in harmony together since the professor's arrival in England, though with very little scientific success. Whenever Grandpa worked hard he became very tired, and when he finally went to bed and fell asleep, he became delirious. He had recurrent nightmares of being chased by windmills, of mad millers running down windy tunnels trying to take him away in their bags. Grandpa slept on a living-room sofa which at night could be changed into a bed. Sometimes, during the night, while Grandpa slumbered in the Land of Nod, he would imagine that the bed was trying to turn back into a sofa again, with him still in it. He would wake up screaming and thrashing his arms about the place, as if he was being devoured by strange monsters. Once they had been wakened up in this manner, both Snaps and the professor found it very hard to get back to sleep again, so they would lie in their beds just waiting for the dawn.

And if night-time with Grandpa was no joke, then daytime was no better. For example, there had been that awful day when Grandpa and Snaps went to the launderette. *High Jinx*, the trailer, had every modern convenience. Being a good forty feet long, it had been remodelled in such a way as to provide the maximum storage space for all sorts of strange equipment, most of it scientific. Yet it lacked one important commodity – a washing machine. And what with all the time Grandpa and the professor spent on endless scientific experiments, there was an endless supply of grimy and greasy overalls to be washed. So one morning Grandpa and Snaps gathered the whole lot up in a huge black polythene bag and headed for the launderette.

Now, Grandpa Kelly had seen an awful lot of the world. Some would even say that, during his more lunatic moments, he had even been to the moon, but that's another story . . . However, he had *never* been to a launderette. Usually, he washed his own miserable shirts at home and hung them out on the TV aerial to dry. When they became too dirty to wash, he simply dyed them a different colour. On one occasion (it was a hot summer's day) he dyed a pair of worn denim dungarees, but all the dye ran down on to his bare feet. After that, he dyed his clothes with his boots on.

Actually, it was Grandpa Kelly who invented born-again denim, but that's another story also . . .

Anyway, Grandpa's first visit to a launderette was a day to remember. Ten o'clock in the morning found him standing in front of a huge washing machine wondering what to do next. The dials on the machine looked like the instrument panel on a Concorde; Grandpa didn't know whether to do his laundry or hijack the thing and fly back to India. Of course, Snaps knew how to operate the machine. In fact, it was he who most usually did the laundry. But on this occasion, Grandpa insisted on doing everything himself. And that's where the trouble began.

Firstly, he couldn't find where the money went in. When he eventually located the slot (which was right under his nose) he jammed it up with a bent ten-pence piece, so that the laundry engineer had to open up the machine to take it out again. Once the machine got going, Grandpa settled down a bit. He was fascinated to see his clothes spinning round like bronco riders in the arena of an American rodeo. He pulled up a chair to the glass door, and sat shouting and cheering as if he were watching a TV western. As soon as the show was over, he inserted more money and started it up again. It would give the clothes a thorough washing, he said. Besides, he wanted to see the ending again.

Meanwhile, as Grandpa was enjoying his second viewing, the large lady who was waiting to use the machine was becoming very angry. She was accompanied by three small and very troublesome babies, and she was far from feeling amused. She kept her patience as best she could until the end of the second run, but when Grandpa inserted more money to start the programme yet again, her patience just ran out.

She sprang to her feet, and let Grandpa have it from both barrels. 'When,' she asked, 'were you let out of the lunatic asylum?' (not an irrelevant question). Then she lambasted him with talk of women's rights, mothers' rights and a lot of other rights besides. Finally, she asked him had he no respect for small innocent babies, had he no feeling at all for the poor innocent things? When she had finished, she sat down again, tired and panting.

You've heard of *solar* power? Well, Grandpa Kelly worked on *lunar* power, like a life-size *Action-Man* that was wired to the moon. (There is, in fact, a lunar crater named after him. Indeed, the Kelly Crater is quite well known, and is clearly visible on most moonlit nights.)

Grandpa glared at the lady with his red guinea-pig's eyes. Then he told her to stop panting, because pants were not allowed in this launderette. With regard to his ideas on babies, they were simply this: all babies should be sent to some remote twilight-zone, where they could piddle and snivel to their little hearts' content. Then he added:

'If you disagree with my ideas, don't complain to *me*. See the storks.'

Of course, all this time the machine was still running, and when Grandpa opened the glass door, sudsy water sploshed all over the floor. But Grandpa was un-disturbed.

'Let's go, Snaps,' he said. 'It looks like the tide is coming in . . .'

As he gathered up his bundle of soggy overalls and his assorted garments of denim (most of it, at this stage, born-again), Grandpa sat for a moment on a chair just inside the launderette door, just above water-level. Snaps suddenly heard a hard snap-crackle-pop, like the sound of a monster *Rice Krispie* being crunched by a crocodile.

'What was that?' said Snaps.

Grandpa stood up slowly. Beneath him was the bony laundry cat who had gone to sleep under the cushion. The poor creature was a little dazed, but none the worse for wear (though its face now looked as if it had been put on backwards). To make amends, Grandpa insisted on taking the poor chap to McDonald's, to treat it to a hearty meal.

'One fishburger,' he said to the attendant. 'Hold the bun, and light on the tartar sauce.'

'Have a nice day,' said the attendant.

'Meeow,' said the cat. (His face was now the right way round.)

'Grandpa, you're bananas!' said Snaps.

'Let's split!' said Grandpa.

So, you can now understand why Snaps was feeling rather down-in-the-mouth as he headed across the park that day with Julie. Nothing seemed to be going right lately. Nothing. In fact, things seemed to be getting steadily worse. When they arrived at the trailer, Snaps and Julie discreetly went inside.

'More high jinx now, I suppose,' Snaps said to himself. But he was wrong. Grandpa and the professor were sitting at the microscope. They were both very silent and they looked a little pale. Snaps sensed that something was wrong. Even Fitzroy had a solemn expression: disappointment clung to his whiskered face the way a bad dream clings to a crumpled pillowcase.

'Bad luck,' the professor announced. 'Take a look in here. I had a feeling that something like this could happen. There's no knowing what might happen next.'

Snaps closed one eye and looked into the microscope at the fragments of half-eaten paper. He could see thousands of dark tiny bodies swimming around.

'What are those things?' he asked. Undigested doubts began to wobble in his tummy.

'The paper-monsters,' answered the professor coldly.

'But I thought they were invisible?'

'They *were*. But not any more. They've started to grow out of all proportion.'

Snaps was flabbergasted, stunned, amazed.

'Gosh! But what happens if they don't stop growing. I mean, if they keep on becoming more and more visible, until we can actually see them crawling around?'

'Let's hope that never happens. In the mean time, we've got to think of ways to make sure that it doesn't. We've got to find a way to stop them; we mustn't stop experimenting. But it's all so mysterious and unknown, like wandering through the dark.'

The professor sighed. He had the frustrated look of someone who was slowly running out of ideas. His brain was tired and empty, like a bus terminal at night.

'So what do we try now?' asked Julie. 'The rocket theory again?'

'Yes, I suppose so,' answered the professor. 'We'll try it once again. Who knows, maybe this time the miracle will happen.'

The rocket theory sounded like it should work, but so far it hadn't. The professor had reckoned that the only way to stop the paper-monsters was to expose them to their natural predators, the paper-scorpions he had brought from the Indian forest in his bagful of leaves. He referred to these creatures as his 'White

Knights' because, he thought, only they could stop the terrible progress of the monsters. But to be really effective, the paper-scorpions had to be sent through space, to be transformed by the mysterious force of speed into something more powerful, just as the paper-monsters had been. Otherwise there would be no contest; the White Knights would be no match for the paper-monsters.

Grandpa and the professor had made a makeshift rocket. It was small (only about one metre high) and awkward-looking, but it was very powerful all the same. Late one night, they had all helped to transport it to a shrubby corner of the park. It flew excellently when Grandpa lit the fuse, high into the night sky at the speed of a real rocket. In all, the space flight lasted about half an hour, not very long really, but the professor thought it might be enough.

It wasn't. They retrieved the sealed box of White Knights from the rocket and sprinkled them over a small piece of unaffected paper. They hoped that the Knights might now be powerful enough to protect the paper from attack. But they weren't, and in the morning the paper was dry and crumbly, as if it had not been treated at all.

The professor tried the experiment again. Maybe the speed of the rocket hadn't been fast enough, or the space journey long enough. The second rocket was bigger, therefore, and more powerful than the first. Once again, they all headed across the park under cover of darkness, pushing a strange-looking object in front of them. Once again the White Knights were on board, and this time Grandpa included a banana as well. Perhaps the banana might undergo some change also. They stepped back behind a bush as Grandpa lit the fuse. The rocket zoomed up faster than ever and was soon a tiny dot in the sky. The space trip lasted about fifty minutes, not that long really, but a good deal longer than the first flight all the same. Once again, they did the paper experiment, and once again it failed. As for the banana, Grandpa left it outside all night on the bonnet of the lorry, hoping that something interesting might happen. But when he went to investigate it in the morning, he found only the banana skin and a message on the windscreen which said: 'Enjoyed banana. Thanks a lot.'

The rocket experiment was now to be tried for a third time. This time, Grandpa and the professor had built the most powerful rocket of all. It was a full two-and-a-half metres high, and had ten times the rocket-booster of the previous models. It also weighed about half as much as a small steam-roller so it was quite difficult to transport. Grandpa named it *Scorpius*, after the starry constellation that ignites the summer sky. (Grandpa liked to nickname things.) Also, just for good luck, he painted a giant scorpion on the side of the fuselage. That night, as they pushed their heavy load towards its launching pad in the corner of the park, Snaps, Julie, Grandpa and the professor all had the feeling that *this was it*. If they failed this time, well what would be their next move? None of them really knew . . .

They had camouflaged *Scorpius* with bushy branches, behind which they hid. Anyone who happened to be passing through the park at that late hour would have seen a huge bushy shrub moving mysteriously over the grass.

Once again they ran for cover as Grandpa lit the

fuse. There was the usual huge burst of fire and noise as the rocket took off, only this time the explosion was more powerful than ever.

'There she blows!' shouted Grandpa as *Scorpius* flashed over the trees, over the city, towards the distant stars. In seconds, it had become a speck of light. Then it vanished.

They sat in silence, huddled together on a park bench, waiting for *Scorpius*'s return. But by three o'clock there was still no sign of it. The professor was puzzled. 'Perhaps we used too much booster,' he thought. 'Or perhaps it got pulled into a planet's gravity field. Or maybe it just exploded miles away in space, where its scattered fragments will be for ever suspended . . .'

They waited in silence for another hour, but there was still no sign of their rocket. Then, as the first crack of oyster light was breaking over the city, they decided to head for home. They trod wearily over the damp morning grass with a heavy feeling of disappointment in their hearts. Snaps was feeling very low indeed . . . Once back at the trailer, he fell into his small bed, and lost himself in the comfortable security of sleep.

It was well past breakfast-time when he finally awoke. Grandpa was exploring the sky through a pair of monster binoculars, but there was still no sign of *Scorpius*. The professor was peering into the microscope. Julie was watching a news item on Grandpa's portable telly. The news item said that the government was offering a reward of ten thousand pounds (in fifty-pence pieces) to anyone who could find a remedy for the growing paper problem. Experts had been flown in from all over the world, but so far no major breakthrough had been made. In the mean time, a well-known Irish rock-star had flown to London where he started a scheme called *Paper-Aid*. A huge pop-concert was arranged in Wembley, where all the bands would give their services free. The money raised at the concert was to go towards the study of the new disease called *paperitis*, a disease that was totally unheard of only a short time ago. Other concerts were to be arranged throughout Europe for the eradication of this disease. In Brussels, EEC officials agreed to release a few tons of paper from their paper mountain. These would go towards the relief of the paper famine in London. Meanwhile, the British Army was being kept on full alert throughout the city (not that the soldiers could do anything, really; it just made people feel better to know that they were there).

'Wow! This *Paper-Aid* idea is really catching on!' Julie said as she switched off the telly. 'It's nice to know that someone cares.'

'But it just might be too late,' said the professor, straightening up from the microscope. 'Take a look here.' His voice was dark and crumbly, like old chocolate. Julie looked down the powerful lens and focused. Dark swimming objects came into view.

'Those are the paper-monsters, aren't they?'

'Yes,' said the professor. 'That's the same sample of paper as yesterday . . .'

'But they look sort of bigger today.' Julie watched the swimming figures closely. What looked like small head lice only yesterday, now had the appearance of swelled ticks.

'Yes, they're still growing,' explained the professor. 'But not only that, they are also transforming their shape. Look closely. You can see tiny extensions on their sides.'

Julie scrutinized one of the swimming monsters. The professor was right. There *were* tiny extensions on their sides.

'Sort of like primitive wings,' she said.

'Exactly!' said the professor. 'That's exactly what I think they are.'

Snaps and Grandpa came to take a look. The professor continued talking.

'Can you imagine what would happen if these creatures developed wings?'

'We're just going to have to confront Gripp,' Snaps said. 'We must go down to Greenwich and face him. He's got to have some sort of remedy. Otherwise, why would he have started all of this? It just wouldn't make sense!'

'But wait a minute,' said Julie. 'That would be very dangerous. This guy is obviously crazy. Remember what happened last time. He nearly killed you and Grandpa!'

'She's right, you know,' said Grandpa, feeling the remains of the bump on his head. 'We can't put the professor's life in danger.'

'Maybe it's time we went to the police,' said Julie.

'No,' objected the professor. 'I will do whatever I can to help. I am not afraid of this man. He was once my friend.'

'Yes, but he's changed now,' said Snaps. 'He's surrounded by an army of goons, not to mention those vicious monkeys.'

'It doesn't matter,' said the professor quietly. 'I will go.'

'We will *all* go,' added Grandpa. 'We're all in this together. All for one and one for all, just like whatever-you-call-them!'

With renewed enthusiasm, they set out for Greenwich. They were huddled together in the cab of the lorry, and Grandpa was at the wheel. Snaps asked him to drive fairly normally, so as not to attract attention. The streets were rather quiet for early afternoon. At each corner soldiers stood in complete battle gear, their faces harassed and worried. The whole city had an air of depression and gloom.

Presently they arrived at Greenwich. Grandpa parked not far from Gripp's house, while Snaps went to investigate.

To his surprise, the small door leading on to Dr Gripp's garden was not locked, and it opened with a slight push. He peered inside. There seemed to be a lot of activity up at the house. He could hear the loud sound of voices, and the slamming of doors. Three huge cars were drawn up on the driveway, with sun-glassed toughies inside them. Then Snaps saw Dr Gripp come hurrying from the house and get into the middle car. Then all three cars started up, in an awful hurry, by the looks of them. They drove down the driveway towards the main entrance. 'They're leaving!' thought Snaps. 'They're getting away! We must stop them!'

His heart was pounding as he dashed back to where Grandpa and the others were waiting. Snaps waved and shouted as soon as he came in sight of Grandpa's truck. 'They're getting away! They're getting away! We must hurry!'

Grandpa started up the engine as soon as Snaps was

safely aboard. It spluttered and stalled. Grandpa tried again. 'Come on, baby,' he muttered. 'Don't let me down now!' He tried again. The whole cab shuddered as the huge engine burst into life. Grandpa let out a cheer of delight, like a cowboy who'd just won his first rodeo: 'Yahoooo! Here we go!' They set off in hot pursuit. Grandpa grinned like an encyclopedia salesman who was moving in for the kill.

'Which car's Gripp in?' he screeched, trying to make himself heard over the roar of the engine as it took up speed.

'The middle one!' Snaps shouted back, pointing to the three black limos that darted away ahead of them.

'We're gaining on them! Keep your boot to the floor, Grandpa!'

There was no need to tell Grandpa Kelly to keep his boot to the floor! He was an expert at dealing with these situations. The limousine is a powerful car, one of America's best. But it is no match for a monstrous artic, especially one that is almost empty, and has no cumbersome load to hinder it. Grandpa's big baby was gobbling up the road, weaving its way with the skill of a soccer player from one lane to another. He was now breathing down the bumper of the last limousine. He gave it a little nudge, just to show that he meant business.

The driver of the limousine felt the thud and he and the other goons looked round. They got an awful fright when they saw Mount Everest on wheels behind them. They took off down the fast lane with the speed of Diego Maradonna, and signalled to the other two cars to follow. Dr Gripp glanced around, and for a split second Grandpa glimpsed the white of his terrified eyes. This was not the same Gripp who had confidently imprisoned Grandpa and Snaps, setting his vicious little moneys upon them. Now he looked anxious and worried.

Grandpa took up his radio microphone and started talking:

'This here's Elvis Kelly, the Hottest Trucker in the West End. Request assistance immediately. Three tins of black sardines speeding through Eastcheap to private butterfly pad. Please intercept. Over.'

Grandpa listened. The radio spluttered and squeaked, but no one answered. He called his message again. Still no reply. Then he remembered. It was Sunday. Maybe there were no truckers working. If not, he would have to do it all alone. The airstrip came into view. Time was running out. He would have to act fast.

The three cars had turned off the motorway on to the small road that led down to the private airstrip, and soon they were speeding along the runway with Grandpa's lorry on their tails. Up ahead there was a large hangar where, Grandpa guessed, Gripp's plane was waiting. He could see that the huge door was already open. The cars turned sharply into the hangar, the rubber of the scorched tyres burning on the hot cement. Grandpa turned also, but the big lorry was awkward, and not easily manoeuvred.

Grandpa did his best to try to control it, but the lorry drove relentlessly onwards until it was brought to a sudden halt by smashing into the far wall of the hangar.

'Oh, no!' roared Snaps, as he saw the wall come up to meet him.

'Hold tight!' screamed Julie.

'God save us!' shouted the professor.

'Someone save us!' shouted Grandpa.

'Mee-OWWWW!' shouted Fitzroy, as his head cracked against the windscreen.

Everyone was stunned. Grandpa escaped the lightest. After all, he was wearing his World-War II helmet. He looked at the others. They were moaning, but at least they were still alive. Grandpa climbed out of the cab. There seemed to be smoke and dust everywhere, and the smell of burning rubber. He gazed into the mist. Presently, a number of shadows appeared before him. He peered again. There were nine of them. Dr Gripp was still in the car. He stared at Grandpa. His eyes were mean and filled with rage. He looked at the nine standing goons and said dryly: 'Get him . . .' Only one of the goons was still wearing sun-glasses. Slowly, he removed them, and folded them into his top pocket. Then all nine started to walk towards Grandpa.

As you probably know by now, Grandpa was usually afraid of nothing. Besides, he had a black belt in karate (and a black suit at the cleaners). Still, nine fat goons against one skinny Grandpa are rather tricky odds, would you not say? His black belt was of no particular use to him at the moment (except, of course, for holding up his trousers). And by the looks of things, he would be needing his black suit pretty soon – to wear to his own funeral. He stepped slowly backwards, looking towards the cab of the crashed lorry.

'Snaps,' he called. 'Snaps, ol' pal. Your grandpa's in a spot of bother . . .'

But Snaps didn't hear him. He and the others were still seeing stars.

Grandpa tried to remember the enemy-avoidance

techniques he'd learned in Korea. Could he pull off a combat-run out of the hangar door? But behind him the doors of the hangar had already been closed.

'Couldn't we behave like civilized people?' Grandpa said, cheerfully. 'After all, this *is* forever England . . .'

The first thump was the worst. It caught Grandpa right in the stomach and it was very sore. He fell over like a sack of spuds. Then one of the goons grabbed him and lifted him up again. A smart box on the jaw sent Grandpa to the floor. He could feel one of his gold-filled molars become very loose. Then they lifted him up again . . .

For a while, Grandpa tried to fight them off, lashing thumps in all directions. But there were just too many of them, so he decided to play dead. When a fist caught him over the eye he fell to the floor and lay quite still, though he wasn't *that* hurt really. His eyes were only half closed.

Gripp got out of the car and walked slowly towards him. He tipped Grandpa's face with his shoe. He seemed quite dead. Then Gripp glanced towards the cab of the lorry. There was no movement from there either.

'OK, let's go!' he said as he headed for the waiting jet plane. 'Open the door!'

Grandpa eyed up at them. They were boarding the plane, escaping. But what could he do? He couldn't tackle nine of them. Not at his age. Well, at least he had done his best . . .

Three of the goons headed for the huge door of the hangar. Behind them, the plane's engines were already whirring. In a matter of seconds, they would all be away, gone, vanished into thin air . . . Grandpa sighed.

closed his eyes once more, and dropped his head on to the cool floor of the hangar.

Then, just before the goons reached the door, it was smartly opened, and three long shadows spread across the floor . . . Grandpa lifted his head and peered into the brightness. It was Big Eddie and, better still, he had brought a couple of very big friends.

'OK, where's my pal Elvis Kelly?' said Big Eddie, and his face looked mean and cruel. He took a few steps into the hangar. Slowly, the three giant lorry-drivers came forward. Then Big Eddie caught a glimpse of Grandpa lying on the ground. He lost his head completely.

'What!' he shouted. 'Pick on an old guy, would you, eh? Well, try me for size!' He lunged forward, his great right arm swinging like Excalibur. In two minutes Big Eddie took care of three of the goons. They were no problem at all. He could handle them easily, with one arm behind his back even. His two giant pals took care of the other six. Soon there was a pile of star-gazing criminals sitting on the floor, waiting to be delivered to the nearest police station.

'Well, that takes care of that little problem,' said Big Eddie. 'You all right pal?'

'Sure am,' said Grandpa, getting up off the floor. 'And thanks. You just came in the nick of . . .'

BANG! A shot rang out and echoed around the hangar. Dr Samuel Gripp stepped from the plane. He was holding a loaded pistol, and he had that mad look in his eyes.

'Nobody comes near me, or I'll shoot!' he said, stepping backwards towards the door. 'I mean it! I'll shoot the first person that moves!'

There was the sound of movement in Grandpa's lorry. Gripp cast his ferret eyes in that direction.

'Come out of there slowly,' he called. 'And don't try any tricks.'

He nearly died of fright when Professor Chaudhuri stepped from the cab.

'Hello, Sam,' said the professor calmly. 'It's been a very long time.'

Dr Gripp was speechless. His hand dropped a little, and his mouth was open. Then he instantly recovered his composure.

'Don't come near me. I'll shoot. Stay where you are!' The professor came slowly forward.

'You saved my life once. Remember? I don't believe you'd really shoot me now.'

'Yes I would. Stay back. I'm getting out of here!'

'And where are you going to go? Forget it, Sam. It's finished. Now give me the gun.' He held out his hand, slowly, carefully.

Gripp stared into the eyes of his old friend and teacher. There was silence for an instant, then he handed the pistol to the professor. His face was no longer wild, only sad and pitiful. Lids drooped like paper-wrappers over his eyes. He handed the professor the pistol.

'They're only blanks,' he said. 'I was never much good with firearms . . .'

– 16 –

Witches' Broom

'Hey, you can't go in there.'

Grandpa brushed aside the two Scotland Yard police-men, as if they were toy soldiers guarding Hamleys' toyshop.

'Course I can,' said Grandpa. 'Who's going to stop me?'

Snaps, Julie and the professor followed him into the office. An outraged Detective Jenkins looked at them in amazement.

'Who are you?' he asked.

Grandpa sat on the edge of the office desk, selected a huge cigar from the cigar box, lit it, looked down at Detective Jenkins and said:

'We're those good citizens who arrested Dr Gripp yesterday. We've come to talk to him.'

'About what?' asked Detective Jenkins.

'The paper-monsters, of course,' said Grandpa, giving the detective a look you could spread on a bun.

'We still haven't proven that Dr Gripp is in any way connected with the recent . . . er . . . occurrences in the city, with regard to the disappearance of paper and sundry other articles made therefrom.' The detective spoke with the authority of a schoolboy who had just swallowed the school dictionary.

'Course he's connected,' snapped Grandpa. 'It's as plain as the nose on your face . . .' (The nose on Detective Jenkins's face *was* quite plain.) 'Anyway, whether he's guilty or not doesn't really matter. It's finding a cure, *that's* what's important now. So, we must see him immediately, if not sooner.'

Grandpa blew expert smoke rings into the air. The detective looked distressed.

'I'm afraid that's impossible,' he said.

'But *we must* . . .' Snaps, Julie and the professor repeated.

'Well, I'm afraid you can't,' said the detective. 'Because he's not here.'

'You mean you've taken him somewhere else,' said Grandpa. 'That doesn't matter. Just tell us where like a good chap, and we'll go to see him wherever it is.'

'I'm afraid you don't understand. Dr Gripp has escaped.' The detective's cheeks were as red as a schoolboy's who has just been caught playing truant. (His nose, however, was still quite plain.)

'Escaped?' A choir of voices sang in unison.

'Yes, escaped.' The detective touched his scorching cheeks with quivering fingers of shame.

'What do you mean "escaped"?' asked Grandpa. 'He was arrested only yesterday. This *is* Scotland Yard, isn't it? I mean, it's not one of those silly American police departments where prisoners can come and go as they please?' Detective Jenkins was shocked and horrified at the audacity of this suggestion. He gave Grandpa a look he usually reserved for criminals.

'Most certainly not,' he said, spitting out the words as if they were being released from captivity.

'How did it happen?' Snaps asked. 'How did Gripp escape so quickly?'

'He's obviously a very organized chap,' said the detective. 'He obviously has friends on the outside, friends who went into action as soon as they heard he had been arrested.' Detective Jenkins stood up. 'Follow me,' he said.

He took Grandpa and his band of three down to the cells, and he showed them the cell where Dr Gripp had been kept overnight. A gigantic hole had been blown through the wall.

'Wow,' said Snaps. 'What caused that?'

'Plain old-fashioned dynamite,' said Detective Jenkins. 'We subsequently found two sticks of it in an abandoned Toyota a few streets away. This was the get-away car presumably. The entire incident is very embarrassing. I still haven't figured out what to say to the public. Still, there were no serious injuries. An anonymous caller tipped us off seconds before the dynamite exploded.'

'You mean you *knew* there was dynamite in the building?' Grandpa asked.

'Yes,' said the detective.

'And you still did nothing about it? You just let the suspect escape?'

'Hey, wait a minute,' protested Jenkins. 'There just wasn't time to do anything. Anyway, it would have been too dangerous. You obviously get your knowledge of explosives from watching TV cartoons. All those farmyard animals and house pets exploding TNT in each others' faces. Well, real bombs do more than burn your fur off. And there's no Hollywood cartoonist to put you back together again in the next frame. Dynamite's not some cheap custard-pie in the paws of a vengeful coyote. And it's not just a practical joke.'

'All right, all right,' said Grandpa. 'There's no need to make excuses. Actually, I'm something of an expert with explosives myself . . .' He took a stick of dynamite from inside his jacket and lit its fuse from the burning end of his cigar. There was a loud gasp as everyone dived for cover. But Grandpa just grinned as he watched the fuse hiss and sizzle.

'Ha, ha. Fooled you all,' he said. 'This is just a toy dynamite I bought in Hamleys'.' He threw the stick through the hole in Dr Gripp's cell. A few seconds later, there was a loud bang, and clouds of falling mortar dust filled the air.

Grandpa coughed and spluttered, lost in a mass of smoke.

'At least, I *thought* that was the one I bought in Hamleys',' he said.

'What happens now?' Snaps asked as they drove back towards Fitzroy Square, their old home.

'I don't know,' answered the professor. 'I just don't know.'

'Where could Dr Gripp be, I wonder?' Julie said. 'More likely than not, he's left the country, I suppose.'

Grandpa said nothing. He just kept driving. But Snaps could see him thinking through the back of his head; he could hear the click of Grandpa's old brain trying to find conclusions. Meanwhile, in his own head, questions were popping like corn in a pan.

Grandpa's latest motor vehicle was an old Post-Office van which he had picked up cheaply somewhere. There were no seats in the back of it, so Snaps and Julie had to sit with their legs stretched out in front of them, but they didn't really mind. That was the least of their worries at the moment.

As they drove past the old paper-mill in Pimlico, there were hundreds of people gathered outside the main gate trying to squeeze their way into the yard. This was one of the centres that was chosen for the distribution of the relief paper that had been brought in from Europe. Grandpa stopped the van and got out to take a look. The ball of people that rolled round the yard was frantic with expectation. Most of them hadn't seen a newspaper, comic or magazine in months, so they were determined not to let this opportunity escape them.

Grandpa climbed the railings, and made straight for the big heavy doors. He pushed, shoved and panted through the swaying sea of bodies, and eventually found himself inside. The papers were laid out on long counters around which flocked people of all ages, like gulls around a council tip. The scene was like the first day of Harrods' sale. Everyone was pulling, snatching, grabbing, trying to take away as much paper as they could. Grandpa managed to come away with ten *Tintin* annuals, a book of *Asterix* cartoons, some football magazines in German, a map of Julius Caesar's travels, a paper bag made in Holland, and last year's calendar.

'Gee, you got quite a lot!' said Julie when Grandpa had returned to the van. Grandpa flicked through the magazines.

'It's berloody murder in there,' he said. 'Anyway, I don't know what all the excitement is about. Who's able to read this stuff? Might as well feed it straight to the monsters!'

'Don't worry,' sighed the professor. 'They'll get it soon enough!'

With that, an old lady burst from the crowd, climbed the railings and went running down the street on legs that were as skinny as stilts. She was carrying a six-pack of pink toilet-rolls, obviously made in France. One of the officials from inside the paper-mill squeezed through the crowd, and chased after her.

'Hey, come back! You can't have all of those!' he called.

However, the old lady escaped by hopping on a bus.

'Ha! Ha! Fooled you!' she shouted at the official, as the bus disappeared round a corner in cartoon clouds of dust.

'Now that's what I admire,' said Grandpa. 'A woman with spirit. Nice legs too . . .' He let out the clutch, and drove off towards Fitzroy Square.

Days passed. Since their return to Fitzroy Square (there was no need to hide themselves away in *High Jinx* any more) Grandpa and the professor had been experimenting frantically. Grandpa had made a new laboratory, where he and the professor did experiments almost all day long. As soon as they got up in the morning they would head in there, and they wouldn't come out again until after dark. Julie helped out whenever she could, and Snaps did errands, usually a trip to the chemist for an urgently-needed powder, liquid or gooey concoction.

'Now let's see what effect this stuff has,' the professor said one day, as he put a strange liquid under the microscope and peered down the lens. He could see nothing but blurs. He adjusted the lens upwards to a higher, more intense reading. Still nothing. Then he adjusted it downwards, to its lowest magnification. What he saw made his blood curdle. The paper-monsters came into focus, much bigger and more terrible than before. They were now just outside the range of naked-eye vision. One more transmutation, and they would be horribly, terribly visible. The professor went straight to his bench and lit the bunsen burner.

'Mix up some more ammonia with SO_5,' he said to Grandpa. 'We've got to work fast.'

Meanwhile, Snaps and Julie went up on to the flat roof of the building. The evening promised, like all others, to be an autumnal sun-bath under a blue dome.

Julie went to Grandpa's telescope, which was poised randomly on its tripod, pointing nowhere in particular. She took it steadily in hand, and the two powerful prisms came to life. She focused out over the roof-tops and chimney-pots. A distant TV aerial appeared before her like a giant H.

'Wow! This thing is really powerful!' Julie said. She turned down on to the street below. An old man slept on a bench in Fitzroy Square. He seemed so close she could almost hear him snoring. Behind him, a scruffy youngster was unwrapping a bar of chocolate. 'That's odd,' Julie said. 'Now where did he get that, I wonder? Hey Snaps, come and take a look.' Snaps came over and squinted through the telescope. The boy had completely unwrapped his bar of chocolate, and had dropped the wrapping paper on the street. Wrapping paper! It couldn't be! Snaps zoomed in on to the precious item on the ground.

'I've got to find him!' he said, as he disappeared inside.

Snaps looked hastily for the paper wrapper the boy had dropped. He just managed to grab it before the breeze blew it down a gully. Yes, it was paper all right, real live paper.

Snaps ran round the corner, just in time to see the small boy come out of *Portland Food and Wine*, the self-service shop beside Portland Road tube-station.

'Hey! You!' he called. 'I want to talk to you! The chocolate. Where did you get it?'

'The chocolate?' said the boy, in a surprised voice. 'I bought it!'

'Where?'

'In Mr Grubb's shop in Willoughby. Just round the corner from where I live.'

'Willoughby? Where's that?'

The boy gestured vaguely.

'North side. Not too far. The 79A goes up that way.'

In a flash, Snaps headed for the bus-stop.

Georgie Grubb's sweet-shop was like something out of Charles Dickens. It was situated at the end of a cobbled lane, and had those thick sort of windows, like the bottoms of glass bottles. On the outside, it looked drab and dull, and seemed permanently closed. But inside, it was an unexpected, scintillating treat. It had an old-fashioned counter with rows of funny-shaped jars filled with lollipops, and there were twisted paper cones of boiled sweets. In one corner stood a Christmas tree, and the whole shop was simply covered with indoor plants. But what really excited Snaps's attention was the collection of chocolates and sweets, all neatly displayed in their colourful paper wrappers. Snaps picked a chocolate bar from the display unit on the counter. He fingered the wrapper carefully. It seemed, like the chocolate itself, untouched by human hands. No frayed edges, no tell-tale particles of dust that would indicate an attack of paperitis. Behind the door, like an old blind dog, a grandfather clock wagged away the years. And the walls were covered with old posters and handbills announcing sales and theatrical performances of sixty years ago. A calendar hung there, a calendar so old it still believed that Woolwich Arsenal could win the League. The entire shop was like an old abandoned radio, full of secret whispers and silence.

'Can I help you?' George Grubb said, as he came into the shop from a room behind the counter. Three huge cats accompanied him, weaving in and out around his slippered feet. One of the cats, a big ginger one that had an ear missing, leaped into the shop-window and started teasing a big black fly. The fly buzzed like a chainsaw.

'Mr Grubb?' Snaps asked.

'Why, yes. Of course. Who else would I be?' He was a quiet little man with a big bushy moustache, and a pair of round spectacles pushed down to the tip of his nose.

'Actually, I didn't come in to buy anything. Just to ask you a few questions.'

'Yes?'

'How can you explain this? All the paper I mean, when there's not a scrap in all of London?'

George Grubb looked puzzled, but said nothing.

'You know about the paper-monsters, don't you? How come you haven't been hit?'

'Paper-monsters?' said George Grubb. 'Yes, I heard about them on the radio. It's really terrible, that.'

In the room behind the counter, a boiling kettle had begun to whistle.

'I was just about to make some tea, if you'd like to join me?'

Snaps followed George Grubb into the small back room. Snaps sniffed the air. The whole place reeked of garlic. He looked around him. It was the most old-fashioned room he had ever seen.

Mr Grubb hadn't even bothered to take down his Christmas decorations. Clumps of dry, dusty holly jutted up from behind the picture frames, like the sad antlers of last year's reindeer.

'I bet you find it rather strange coming into a room like this,' Mr Grubb said in his chuckly voice as he handed Snaps a cup of tea, 'I bet you think I'm some sort of old dope who's lost his marbles!' It seemed silly to answer 'No', so Snaps just waited for Mr Grubb to continue talking. Mr Grubb poured some tea on to his saucer, lifted it with his delicate fingers, and slurped noisily.

'It's just that I've kept the room exactly as it was when Maevis died.' The chuckle had gone from Mr Grubb's voice, and was replaced by a noticeable sadness.

'Maevis was my wife. That's why I've changed nothing: the plants, the clocks, the Christmas cards and decorations are all exactly as they were the day she died.'

Mr Grubb stopped talking. He reached for a clove of

garlic and popped it into his mouth. The garlic was crushed and flattened by his old yellow teeth, and a strong spray of odour was sent across the room.

'Now, about this other problem, the paper-monsters, I mean. I really don't know how I've managed to escape. Unless, perhaps, that I'm just lucky . . .'

'Perhaps, but somehow I feel it must be more than that . . .' Snaps looked round the room, his eyes searching every object for the trace of a clue. 'There must be something here that keeps the monsters away. Something that they're allergic to.'

'Maybe it's the garlic!' said Mr Grubb as he popped another clove.

'Maybe it is . . .' Snaps looked up. Hanging from the ceiling were strange dark objects, like bats' wings.

'What are those?' Snaps asked.

Mr Grubb adjusted his spectacles and looked at the ceiling.

'Those? Why, some old witches' broom, of course!'

'I beg your pardon?'

'Oh, I am sorry, I meant to say mistletoe. Maevis always called it by its old country name. A beautiful plant, is the mistletoe. But parasitic, I believe. Lives off other plants in the woods and forests.'

'Parasitic? Did you say parasitic?' Snaps's heart was pounding. Perhaps at last he was on to something.

'Yes, parasitic,' said Mr Grubb. 'You know what that means, don't you? A parasite is something that lives off something else. Still, it doesn't seem right that the beautiful mistletoe should be a parasite, does it? OK for those old ones, though; they're not very beautiful any more. A bit dried up and wizened, like myself, I suppose.' Mr Grubb gave his little chuckle.

'You're sure about it being a parasite?' Snaps asked excitedly.

'Why, of course I'm sure. Just look here.' Mr Grubb reached for the big book that lay on the dresser behind him. The book was called *Plants, Shrubs and Flowers of the English Countryside*. Snaps took the book and found the page that said *mistletoe*. Quickly, excitedly, he devoured the words with his eyes:

The mistletoe is an evergreen bush, pale-green in colour, with thick leathery leaves. It is also a parasite, which means that it lives on other plants, usually the apple tree, hawthorn, poplar, willow or oak. There are many superstitions and legends about the mistletoe. It was worshipped in ancient times for its strange magical powers. It is said to have power to dispel the forces of darkness. It has also been used as a strange magical cure for all sorts of illnesses and evils . . .

'Gee!' said Snaps, as he closed the book and handed it back to Mr Grubb. 'Wouldn't it be amazing if . . .' But Snaps didn't bother to finish his sentence. He was afraid to start hoping, just in case he might be disappointed again. He said goodbye to Mr Grubb, then set off to find some mistletoe. On his way out of the shop he noticed that the ginger cat had caught the big black fly . . .

— 17 —

Bright Lake of Darkness

In the large store belonging to Buck and Co., Mr
Buck turned to his assistant and asked: 'Do we have
any mistletoe for this young gentleman?'

'Mistletoe?' repeated the assistant, in a rather surprised voice. 'Why, no sir, we don't have any mistletoe.
Perhaps if the young gentleman would care to come
back in two months . . . Or perhaps he might like to try
Mr Jaeger, the florist.'

Mr Buck looked closely at Snaps, and seemed to
recognize him.

'Weren't you here not so long ago looking for a
Christmas tree?'

'Yes,' said Snaps, 'that was me . . . The Christmas tree
was for a friend. Well OK, thanks a lot.' As Snaps left the
shop, he thought he heard stifled sniggers behind him.

There was no mistletoe at Mr Jaeger's either. So
Snaps decided to go to the one place where there was
sure to be some: in Kew Gardens.

For the second time that evening he crossed the city by bus. The traffic was slow and ponderous; Snaps just about got to the gardens before they closed. He told his story to an old sun-tanned gardener who was quite an expert on trees and shrubs. He took Snaps across the oak lawn and led him to the corner of the gardens where the mistletoe grew. There he carefully snipped off some of the nicest pieces of mistletoe and handed them to Snaps.

'I hope your theory works,' he said.

'Me too,' said Snaps. '*Something* has to . . .' With that, he headed back to the bus-stop to get the bus for home.

There was nobody back at the house in Fitzroy Square when Snaps got there. The laboratory was in semi-darkness, because the blinds were drawn. Grandpa often did this to keep out the sun. Snaps went to the microscope where the infected paper lay like a patient anaesthetized upon an operating-table. It was then he noticed the huge black stain. 'Some spilled ink,' he thought. 'Grandpa is often very clumsy.' Snaps reached for the small desk lamp and flicked it on. The black blob of ink was moving, crawling! It was the paper-monsters! They were visible! The horrible little bodies were wriggling like deformed army ants!

'Holy cow!' shouted Snaps. He looked around desperately for something to gather them into. He picked up a huge glass jar and a silver dagger that had once been used for disembowelling envelopes. He stuck the dagger into the wriggling mass of bodies and carefully lifted. Luckily, they stayed stuck together, like a swarm of bees. He dropped the ugly black ball into the jar and securely sealed the lid. Once they had been dropped on to the bottom of the jar, the monsters separated. They crawled frantically up the sides and across the glass lid. Snaps watched in amazement. It was hard to describe them. He had never seen anything quite so ugly before. They weren't really like ants when you looked at them closely. More like frogs with three pairs of legs. Certainly their heads were the biggest part of them, and he could just about make out the tiny vicious teeth.

'What's going on?' Snaps nearly jumped out of his skin. He hadn't heard Grandpa and the others come in. He said nothing, but pointed at the jar. Three mouths fell open in shocked surprise.

'Blow me down!' said Grandpa.

'Oh, no!' said Julie. 'So it's happened! Now what do we do?'

'I've got an idea,' Snaps said as he placed the clump of mistletoe on the table. Each of them gazed at the mistletoe while Snaps explained his plan.

'Why, that's the craziest idea I've every heard!' said Grandpa. Then he added: 'But let's try it!'

When the monsters had become less restless, Snaps carefully unscrewed the glass lid and quickly dropped the clump of witches' broom inside. Then he instantly closed the jar again. Six pairs of eyes watched the jar closely (the professor was wearing spectacles, and Fitzroy had just come in to see what all the excitement was about).

'Doesn't seem to make any difference,' said Julie.

The monsters continued to crawl around; they were apparently undisturbed by this intruder from the forest.

'Maybe it takes a while to work?' said the professor in a hopeful voice.

'Maybe it doesn't work at all!' said Snaps doubtfully. Then, just as they were about to abandon the experiment altogether, the jar began rocking on the bench with an audible clatter, like a lobster doing a Spanish gypsy dance. Five sets of mouths fell open. Inside the jar, the monsters were going berserk. They ran about frantically, blindly rushing up the sides of the jar, trying to escape from their terrible prison. Their running became more furious, more serious, more desperate. They were not like separate bodies now; more like one swaying mass of chaotic movement. The jar continued to rock danger-ously, and when Snaps put out his hand to steady it, the skin of his fingers was burned by a burst of searing heat.

'Ow!' he shouted. 'The glass is boiling!'

The glass jar fell over on to its side, rolled a bit, then smashed on to the floor.

'Watch out!' shouted Grandpa. 'They're escaping!'

But the monsters stayed in one heaving clump, like a bunch of ugly black grapes. Suddenly, their black beetle bodies cracked open, uncovering blobs of dark jelly. Then they started to sizzle, as if someone had thrown scalding water on them. Their hard legs fell off, and a foul odour filled the room as the wriggling bodies started to melt away. They were decomposing, putrefy-ing, and the ugly smell of their corruption continued to taint the air. As soon as Snaps got his voice back, he let out a tremendous shout.

'It works! It works! I just knew it would!'

The blackness on the floor continued to sizzle and boil. There were sudden small explosions as the last of the beetle bodies cracked, and the dark jelly spilled out. Soon there was no trace of life or movement; just a curious-looking ink stain on the floor.

Snaps continued to stare. He had never in all his life seen such an evil display. The professor too was flabbergasted, and was mumbling softly to himself. Julie stood at Snaps's side. She was feeling a bit scared.

'Well, that's it then,' Snaps repeated, this time in a quieter voice. 'Mr Grubb's witches' broom did the trick after all.'

Grandpa went to the window to let in some fresh air. A stale smell of burning still hung upon the room.

'OK,' said Snaps. 'We've got to spread the good news. Let's first contact the TV and radio stations.'

'Hang on,' objected the professor. 'We're still not sure. We've got to do further tests . . .'

'No time,' Snaps interrupted. 'We've got to act fast. Clumps of mistletoe will have to be hung in every building in London. That's going to take a bit of organizing. Let's go, Julie . . . C'mon professor, and don't worry, I'm sure we're doing the right thing. Hey Grandpa, what's the matter? Can't you get that window open?'

Grandpa was standing with his hands on the window-frame. But he hadn't yet opened it. He slowly turned round and the intensity of his expression sent a cold shiver through the room.

'What's the matter?' asked Snaps. 'What's out there?'

'Anyone here order some small, black, wriggly monsters?' Grandpa said.

'No!' came the unanimous reply.

'No? Well, there's a million of them heading in this direction . . .'

'What?' There was a smart dash for the window. Across the square, a black inky mass was slowly creeping, blotting out the white of the clean road and flag-stones.

'It's hit the fan now,' said Grandpa. 'And just when we thought we had 'em licked!'

'Where did they come from?' Julie asked.

'From just about everywhere,' said the professor. 'The important question now is, where are they heading?'

'Maybe it's a show of strength, a sort of mass rally like what they have in Red Square,' said Grandpa.

'Or maybe they're staging a funeral for their mates,' Snaps added.

'I hope they don't head this way,' said Julie with real terror in her voice. 'Just look at them! Yuk!'

But the massive sea of marching monsters continued onwards, round the corner, and out on to the main street. They were gregarious creatures, like ants or bees, responding to the wild mysterious call of their leader. From every building they poured, from every nook and cranny. They slithered down steps, climbed up from basements and gullies, slid out from under locked doors. They were wild, mad, demented creatures, driven onwards by the ferocious pangs of hunger and thirst. For weeks they had been devouring every available scrap of paper in London, and during that time they had grown and increased rapidly. But now their food supply had disappeared, so their instincts told them to head back to where leaves and other vegetation were plentiful. That meant heading for the park. They could, of course, have picked any park in London. There would, for example, have been more to devour in Kew Gardens than anywhere else. However, because the first movement of their leader had been towards Hyde Park, they continued steadily in that direction. Hyde Park had food in abundance, and water was plentiful in its wide lake. Also, it held none of that dreaded mistletoe among its trees and shrubs. The extinction of their comrades by the mistletoe's unseen magic had sent a wave of distress calls over the monsters' sophisticated antennae. Their instinct for survival had been instantly activated. They intended not only to survive, but also to triumph.

'What do we do now?' asked Julie, her eyes never leaving the black swarm that was continuing its terrible march on the streets of London.

'Nothing,' said the professor. 'We're beaten . . .'

'Like 'ell we are,' said Grandpa, turning away from the window. 'C'mon folks, let's go. We'll head them off at the canyon!'

'We'll what?' shouted Snaps. But Grandpa didn't hear him. He was already in the lift, waiting for the others to join him.

Meanwhile, in Oxford Street, traffic had screeched to a halt, as the monsters continued their relentless march towards the park. They swarmed over cars, buses and taxis. People screamed and became hysterical as the strange deformed creatures scrambled over their shoes. Everyone rushed into shops, trying to get on to higher ground. Some people even stood on up-turned dustbins in an attempt to keep clear of the terrible sea of insects. Motorists panicked, abandoning their cars in the middle of the road, and tried to clamber over the crunching, squelching, bodies. Soldiers stood well back into doorways watching the slow black tide surge past them. They were speechless and confused, holding their weapons at the ready, but not knowing how to use them against such a strange enemy. The police were bewildered and, like everyone else, quite scared. They didn't know what to do. So, for the moment, they just ran for cover.

Grandpa decided to take the cab of the artic rather than the PO van. For one thing, he preferred to be well above ground level at this particular moment. He drove down some side-streets with his three faithful companions beside him. (Fitzroy had decided to stay at home.) They were travelling parallel to Oxford Street, and they got intermittent glimpses of the marching monsters through the gaps in the buildings.

At the turn-off for the park there was a major road-block, caused by hundreds of abandoned buses and cars. A policeman in white traffic gear signalled to Grandpa to turn back. 'No way!' said Grandpa, and with that he zoomed on to the hard shoulder towards Lancaster Gate, squashing numerous small cars with the lorry's mighty wheels.

This section of the park was relatively free of monsters. All the action seemed to be over at the other end. Grandpa went in that direction, towards the lake, and the trees. He wondered if the monsters had arrived yet.

They had. They poured through the gates, over the walls, across the acres of grass. They came in their millions, from every corner of London. It was an amazing, blood-curdling sight, watching the black waves cover the land, like a sea being drawn by the unseen pull of gravity. Just when it seemed that the entire number of monsters had arrived, another shapeless cluster would enter the park, as if in answer to some strange unheard command.

It was now evening, and the situation became more

threatening with the gradual approach of night. Over-head, the helicopters had arrived, twirling rather help-lessly in the twilight sky. The Prime Minister made a special appearance on TV, imploring people to remain indoors until the situation was under control. But really, nobody knew exactly what to do.

Grandpa drove right into the park over the swaying bodies until he was completely surrounded by a sea of blackness. Snaps looked through the window of the cab. He had to keep reminding himself that this wasn't just another of his nightmares.

Persistently the monsters, half-crazed and starving, attacked the trees. Leaves and soft twiggy branches disappeared in seconds. The professor's eyes were wide and red, as if he were looking into hell. He had seen many swarms of locusts in his lifetime, millions of insects that could devour vegetation in a matter of seconds, but never anything like this.

'Why don't they use their wings?' Julie asked. 'Why are they crawling instead of flying?' But no one had an answer to that question.

The monsters scrambled up the trunks of trees and demolished the foliage.

Then they attacked another tree, and the process started again. They climbed and feasted, then fell to the ground, their bodies swollen and gorged. When they had finished devouring, they swarmed towards the wide lake to satisfy their thirst. From all sides of the lake they came, entering the water in their millions. They swam out from the shore so as to make room for their comrades who were still arriving at the water's edge. They poured into the lake, continuously, relent-lessly, until the last trace of blackness was cleared from the land. The lake was like a vast reservoir swallowing them up.

Up above, the helicopters had switched on their searchlights and were scanning the surface. In the half-light of evening, Grandpa and the gang could see the mass of swaying bodies moving in the water like great blobs of seaweed. The professor took his binoculars and focused.

'I should have guessed it,' he said. 'Those aren't wings, they're fins. Those creatures are amphibians!'

While the others thought about this terrible announcement, Snaps watched the thousands of soldiers arrive in tanks, lorries and armoured cars. The lake was soon surrounded, and lit up by massive searchlights from both ground and air. Now that it was fairly safe, the TV cameras had arrived, and the Prime Minister was heading for Downing Street. Everyone waited. A stillness hung over the lake, a stillness that was terrible. Then the water began to swell with a sudden burst of movement. Strange, ugly heads appeared and disappeared, then reappeared again.

'Look, Grandpa!' screamed Snaps. 'Look how they've grown. As big as frogs almost. They're transforming themselves again!'

But Grandpa wasn't looking. His eyes were turned towards a strange bright light in the sky. It was over the buildings, over the trees, travelling towards them at an enormous speed. It seemed to be an aircraft of some sort. Closer and closer it came, flying low and hard over the roof-tops. It was burning with a strange red and green glow.

Everyone had spotted it now. The policemen, the soldiers, the people who watched from the tops of buildings, all turned their faces towards the object in the sky.

'What is it?' Snaps asked, but no one answered.

The object was upon them now, flying directly overhead, and they could see its special markings. It wasn't that big really; it was a rather small craft, a sort of missile. The object zoomed in a wide arc and then returned again. As it darted overhead the second time, Grandpa and his gang glimpsed the large word marked on the fuselage, and what they saw nearly took their breath away. It said *Scorpius*! This was their home-made rocket, at last returned from the vast depths of space! A loud cheer burst from Grandpa's lorry. Snaps and Julie hugged each other, while Grandpa bounced up and down on the springy seat. The professor just stared and wondered. A million questions were running through his mind.

Scorpius flew low overhead, turned with the skill of a fighter jet, and then zoomed round in great sweeping movements, making magic circles in the air. Everywhere was touched by the strange red and green glow: the clouds, the trees, even the faces of the people who had come out to watch the bizarre drama unfold. *Scorpius* dipped down over the lake, where the great mass of monsters continued to moon-bathe. The lake was now a lake of darkness lit up by the mysterious glowing light. Here and there, the monsters were starting to scramble back on to dry land. They moved slower now, heavy with their drink. Yet in no time at all their vicious teeth would be ripping through the vegetation until absolutely nothing remained.

Then a spectacular thing happened; not only spectacular, but strange, peculiar, incredible almost.

Scorpius crossed the lake of darkness in great swooping movements. Round and round it went, over and back, to the outer verge and then back again. The fluorescent colour was reflected on the water and remained there, like a permanent effulgent dye. Soon the great well of ink was changed to a swelling sea of bright glowing light. The monsters heaved and scrambled, upset by this intruder from the sky. They were no longer black, but radiated colours of dark red and purple, like shiny kidney beans. The lake churned and swayed with their new burst of movement, as more of them tried to make for the shore. Then, with one final swoop, *Scorpius* dropped a rolling ball of light on to the surface of the water. The ball rolled and swirled for an instant, and then burst into flames. A tremendous burst of unbearable brightness was scattered to the clouds. Those who watched had to shield their eyes from the great wall of flames as the water of the lake caught fire. Here and there, the fire cast out an angry arm to snatch at those monsters who had managed to scramble ashore. It burned for no more than minutes, and ended with the same rapidity with which it had begun. Soon, the night was calm again, with no noise except the quiet sound of lake water lapping on the shore.

People came from their hiding-places, amazed and bemused. Snaps, Grandpa, Julie and the professor walked slowly to the water's edge. When they touched the water, it was clear and cool. It was also cleaner than it had ever been before. The paper-monsters were gone.

Above the roof-tops, high above the city, the strange flying object continued to glow and twinkle. Then it disappeared into the night . . .

– 18 –

Epilogue

It was late October. The last of the mild autumn days
settled peacefully over the city. The schools had opened
once again, and life got back to normal. Julie returned
to work in the library, and Snaps resumed his job at
Pilkington's. In the parks, the last of the leaves were
falling, and the few remaining flowers that fringed the
avenues were turning brown and papery. Little by
little, the litter-bins filled up again with discarded
paper, which spilled out on to the street. But, for once,
the litter was a welcome sight, a happy reminder that
the paper-monsters had gone. Most of the shops on the
high streets were busily preparing for Hallowe'en. Their
windows were stuffed with bangers and rockets and
magnificent cardboard masks. All over London, people
were good-natured and friendly.

Meanwhile, over in Fitzroy Square, Professor Chaudhuri was preparing to return to his home in the Him-
alaya Mountains. This was his last night in England,

so Snaps and Julie had cooked a magnificent curry. As usual, during the meal, they had all talked again about the strange things that had happened in the park. Indeed, this was their only topic of conversation lately. Still, no matter how much they talked and discussed – until late into the night sometimes – the whole affair still remained a mystery.

As they were finishing their last meal together, and as Snaps was carrying in the coffee, who should call to see them but Tom Tibbles, Grandpa's old friend from the police station. He was carrying a small canvas bag.

'Hello G.,' he said to Grandpa. 'I hope you don't mind, but I let myself in.'

'Come in, my friend!' said Grandpa warmly. 'It's great to see you. Sit down. Have some coffee.'

Tom Tibbles sat down.

'Actually, this isn't exactly a social call. I've something here you might be interested in seeing.'

He took a collection of large photographs from the canvas bag and handed them to Grandpa. Grandpa could see at a glance that they were photos of his home-made rocket. On one of the photos, the name *Scorpius* was clearly visible. Grandpa flicked through the collection quickly.

'Why, that's our rocket, isn't it?' he said. 'But where were these pictures taken?'

Tom Tibbles looked worried, as if he had some bad news to tell. He said:

'These photos were taken by a friend of mine, called Bill Tubbs. He used to be in the underwater section of the force, but he's retired now. However, he still does some diving in his spare time; it keeps him active, you know. Anyway, one weekend he was diving down near the mouth of the Thames, where the river runs into the Channel. He saw a large shining object on the sea floor. He swam down to investigate, and found this rocket. He took these photos of it, and also some pictures of other stuff. Lots of strange-looking objects get dumped in the sea. Well, he thought no more about the matter until he saw the TV pictures of the rocket in the park, the one that suddenly appeared out of nowhere.'

'What exactly are you getting at, Tom?' Grandpa asked.

'These photos were taken about a month ago; that would be just about two weeks before the strange appearance of the second airship, or whatever it was.'

'Are you saying that the rocket in the park was not ours?'

'It couldn't have been. Your home-made one had already crashed into the sea . . .'

'But it was identical. In size, shape, name, everything! There must be some mistake. Maybe your friend saw something else.'

'But he took those photos of it, didn't he? That was on the twenty-fifth, two days after your rocket was launched. Anyway, there is something else.'

Tom Tibbles reached again into the canvas bag. He took out a sealed container and handed it to Grandpa.

'My friend retrieved this from the wreck. Have any of you ever seen it before?'

'Why, yes,' said Grandpa. 'We all have. It's the box we used to send the White Knights into space.'

'White Knights?' said Tom Tibbles in a questioning voice.

'Oh, I beg your pardon,' said the professor. 'That is

what we called the paper-scorpions we used in our experiment. They were meant to travel through space and be transformed into powerful creatures . . .'

'Oh, really?' Tom Tibbles said. His voice sounded rather doubtful. Then he continued with his story.

'Anyway, after he had seen the report of the Hyde Park incident on TV, Bill Tubbs decided to return to the site of the wreck, to check out the crashed rocket again. He thought there might be the makings of a story for the press. But the wreck was gone. He searched everywhere, spent a long time down there, until his oxygen ran short, but there was no sign of it anywhere. Course it's possible that it could have been pulled out to sea. Even very heavy objects can be tossed about when the sea gets rough. So it's quite logical that's what happened . . . Well that's the story. What do you make of it all?'

'I don't know,' Grandpa said. 'I just don't know . . .'

'So the rocket in the park wasn't ours after all,' Julie said.

'Or perhaps it was,' said the professor. 'Either way it's still a mystery.'

'Oh well, let's open this container,' said Grandpa. 'Does anyone have the key?'

The professor searched in his waistcoat pocket, took out a small silver key and handed it to Grandpa. The lock turned roughly and clicked open. A tiny trickle of sea water dribbled from the keyhole. The container was empty. Its inside was polished clean as a whistle. No trace of forest leaves, paper-scorpions or 'White Knights'. Nothing.

'That's odd,' said Grandpa, and his face was puzzled. 'Now where could they have gone to?'

'Another mystery,' sighed the professor. His scientific

mind was having a hard time of it lately. Inside his brain, there was standing-room only.

'Maybe it's not a mystery,' said Snaps, who had not spoken since Tom Tibbles began his strange story. 'Maybe there is an explanation. Or at least, a sort of one . . .'

The others looked at him quizzically.

'What do you mean?' Julie asked.

'Oh, I don't know really,' Snaps said. His voice was nervous and faltering.

'It's just that, in the park . . . when *Scorpius* zoomed past us . . . I thought I saw . . . through the small porthole . . .'

'What?'

'I thought I saw . . . Oh, nothing . . . It was probably nothing, really. Just my imagination. Yes, that's what it was. Just my imagination . . .'

BIG IGGY

Kaye Umansky

When large Lizzy decides it's time she had a bit of peace and quiet, Big Iggy – the smallest dragon – and his brothers all take off into the big wide world. But Big Iggy's first flight ends with a crash landing into a tree – and a huge adventure.

WITCHES IN STITCHES

Kaye Umansky

Your very own monster magazine! Jokes, interviews, competitions, quizzes, health and beauty, songs, poems, lonely hearts, horrorscopes, special offers – it's packed with original and totally unexpected fun.

BAGTHORPES LIBERATED

Helen Cresswell

In the seventh book about the eccentric Bagthorpe family, Mrs Bagthorpe is determined to liberate the female members of the household from domestic drudgery and sets out to rally support for her radical views. But a string of hilarious incidents proves all too clearly that if there is one thing Mrs Bagthorpe can never be, it's liberated.

TALES FROM THE SHOP THAT NEVER SHUTS
Martin Waddell

McGlone lives at the Shop that Never Shuts, and Flash and Buster Cook are in McGlone's Gang with wee Biddy O'Hare. In these five highly entertaining stories the Gang dig for Viking treasure, are frightened that a sea monster has eaten Biddy, discover that McGlone needs glasses, look after the Shop that Never Shuts on their own, and give Biddy a birthday party.

VERA PRATT AND THE BALD HEAD
Brough Girling

When Wally Pratt and his fanatic mechanic mother enter the Motorbike and Sidecar Grand Prix, nothing is really as it seems. Vera's old enemy, Captain Smoothy-Smythe, is up to his old tricks and suddenly Wally is kidnapped. Rescue him? She can't do that yet, she's got to win the Grand Prix first. Two minutes to go and Vera finds herself the ideal partner – a headmaster with no hair!

CRUMMY MUMMY AND ME
Anne Fine

How would you feel if your mother had royal-blue hair and wore lavender fishnet tights? It's not easy for Minna being the only sensible one in the family, even though she's used to her mum's weird clothes and eccentric behaviour. But then the whole family are a bit unusual, and their exploits make very entertaining and enjoyable reading.

SANTA'S DIARY

Shoo Rayner

What's life really like for Santa Claus as the build-up begins for Christmas. Meet him, his family, his reindeer and a host of other characters and read his extraordinary personal life story in this amazing never-before-published diary.

RUDOLPH'S CHRISTMAS FUN BOOK

Martyn Forrester

A Christmas activity book – sacks full of Christmas crosswords, quizzes, fax, puzzles, games, jokes and lots of fun things to do instead of watching the Christmas edition of *Neighbours*! This one will sleigh you (ho ho).

GOGGLE-EYES

Anne Fine

Kitty hated Gerald Faulkner from the moment she met him. What her mother saw in him she couldn't imagine. He was quite unlike her father and had nothing in common with any of them as far as she could see, and his goggling at her mother's legs really got on her nerves. But when 'Goggle-Eyes' left after a dramatic quarrel, Kitty was amazed to discover she missed him . . . A thoroughly entertaining, sensitive, sometimes serious but always very funny novel.

MR BROWSER AND THE SPACE MAGGOTS

Philip Curtis

When it rains every playtime for a month and the school field turns brown, Mr Browser and Class 8 of Chivvy Chase School begin to suspect that something odd is happening. But the local Nature Reserve Warden has mysteriously disappeared, leaving behind him strange messages about Space Maggots. Is there anything Selwyn, Anna and Spiky can do to foil the Space Maggots' devilish plan?

WELL, WELL, WELL

Dr Peter Rowan

Find out what your body can (and can't) do; how its many parts work together to keep you healthy; what happens when things go wrong and who and what can make you better. Dr Pete gives some top tips on how to keep yourself (and others) fit, as well as some breath-taking facts about your body which will amaze and amuse you.

THE GREAT PUFFIN JOKE DIRECTORY

Brough Girling

No great directory could start without an aardvark joke. Use this directory to find out what Humpty did with his hat, how to start a jelly race and what the vampire's favourite soup is ... Packed with alphabetical fun to keep you and your friends giggling for years, this is the world's funniest A–Z of jokes.